I didn't hear him approach

I only knew that when I raised my head, the handsomest man I'd ever seen was standing over me, hands in the pockets of his air force dress uniform pants. His head was slightly cocked to one side, a mischievous grin played on his lips, and he was studying me. My heart stopped.

"Running away?" His voice was like warm brandy. He didn't wait for my answer. "Mind if I join you?"

"Are—are you sure?" I stammered.

"Never surer of anything in my life," he said, sitting down beside me. "I've been looking for you."

"For me?"

"I haven't been able to keep my eyes off you all evening."

My breath caught. "Me?" I couldn't think, much less converse, so caught was I in the tremulous quality of the moment.

He slipped an arm around my bare shoulder and turned me toward him. "What I'd really like to do is kiss you."

And he did. All the fireworks and starbursts in the world were tame compared to the immediacy and power of that kiss. When we broke apart, he framed my face, brushed one finger across my cheek and with a lazy smile added, "And now I'm going to do it again."

Dear Reader,

A writer often, wittingly or unwittingly, is influenced by events in her own life. I am no exception. By nature I am nostalgic and sentimental. Artifacts from the past—photographs, a pressed flower from a prom corsage, a birth announcement—transport me to a treasured moment or a special person. So it is with the billiken, which inspired Isabel and Sam Lambert's love story.

The billiken, a small Buddha-esque figurine with a round belly, pixie ears and an impish grin, was the rage from approximately 1909 to 1912. My grandmother kept hers in a china cabinet crammed with dishes, glassware and tiny porcelain dolls. When she died, others took the valuable plates and crystal; I wanted the billiken. It has sat on my desk for forty years, waiting for its story—this story.

The billiken asks the question "What would it mean in life if things were as they ought to be?" Would dreams come true? Can life's dark moment become the way things were destined? Isabel and Sam's relationship is tested by conflict, separation, tragedy and secrets. But in the end, the message is exactly as it should be: true love endures.

Best,

Laura Abbot

P.S. I'd love to hear your reactions to *Stranger at the Door*. Please write me at P.O. Box 373, Eureka Springs, AR 72632, or e-mail me at LauraAbbot@msn.com.

STRANGER
AT THE DOOR
Laura Abbot

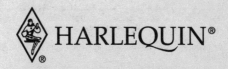

TORONTO • NEW YORK • LONDON
AMSTERDAM • PARIS • SYDNEY • HAMBURG
STOCKHOLM • ATHENS • TOKYO • MILAN • MADRID
PRAGUE • WARSAW • BUDAPEST • AUCKLAND

ISBN-13: 978-0-373-78262-8
ISBN-10:   0-373-78262-4

STRANGER AT THE DOOR

This edition published by arrangement with Harlequin Books S.A.

® and TM are trademarks of the publisher. Trademarks indicated with
® are registered in the United States Patent and Trademark Office, the
Canadian Trade Marks Office and in other countries.

www.eHarlequin.com

Printed in U.S.A.

Books by Laura Abbot

HARLEQUIN SUPERROMANCE

Don't miss any of our special offers. Write to us at the following address for information on our newest releases.

Harlequin Reader Service
U.S.: 3010 Walden Ave., P.O. Box 1325, Buffalo, NY 14269
Canadian: P.O. Box 609, Fort Erie, Ont. L2A 5X3

This book is dedicated
to my special Thursday-morning friends
who are such blessings to me and without whose
unfailing encouragement and unconditional love,
I would be so much the poorer.

Acknowledgments

For detail concerning the United States Air Force
and the experiences of Vietnam-era pilots
and their families, I am deeply indebted to
Lieutenant Colonel Lyle E. Stouffer USAF (Ret)
and Lieutenant Colonel Jack Anderson USAF
(Ret). My thanks go also to their wives, Mary Jo
and Rosemary, for additional insights and help.
Any errors of fact are mine.

PROLOGUE

Breckenridge, Colorado

NERVES ON EDGE, MARK Taylor stood at the top of the driveway studying the large two-story log home shrouded by blue spruce and boasting a view across the tarn of craggy peaks. Unaccustomed to the altitude, he drew a labored breath, concerned that the next few hours would be awkward at best and difficult at worst. However, there was no turning back. For his peace of mind, the meeting was vital. And long overdue.

His strategy was surprise. Otherwise, immediate rejection was too real a consequence. But so was the possibility of shattering a family. He reminded himself it was too late for second-guessing.

The wide front porch, bedecked by hanging baskets, was inviting, serene. He paused, tension rooting him to the spot. Get a grip, he told himself. You're a forty-year-old man, not a six-year-old.

Lungs working overtime in the thin air, he

stuffed his hands into the pockets of his ski jacket and walked toward the massive front door where a woodburned sign above it read Welcome To Lamberts' Lodge. Closing his eyes, he mumbled a quick prayer, then pressed the bell. And waited.

An attractive older woman dressed in khaki slacks and an oversize flannel shirt answered. She looked like a friendly type with short salt-and-pepper hair and laugh lines framing her mouth. "May I help you?" She held the door, poised to shove it closed.

He found his voice. "Mrs. Lambert, is your husband home?" Wariness clouded her expressive brown eyes and she pulled back.

Before she could answer, he went on. "I'm sorry. That question must've alarmed you, and that is certainly not my intent. My name is Mark Taylor. I'm an attorney from Savannah. I'm here to speak with your husband. On a personal matter."

"I'm sorry, Mr. Taylor, but he is unavailable at the moment. Was he expecting you?"

"No, we've never met." Hope warred with a panic he was helpless to control. A chill mountain breeze slithered down his back. "I've come all the way from Georgia. It's important that I talk with him."

"What could possibly be so urgent that you would travel halfway across the country to meet my husband without an appointment?"

He controlled himself with difficulty. "I'd rather not say, ma'am. May I just wait for him?"

"I don't think that's advisable, particularly since I've never heard my husband mention you."

"But you don't understand—"

"No, I don't. I'll tell him you came by, but now you'll have to excuse me." She moved to shut the door.

Momentary dizziness swept over him and involuntarily the words spilled forth. "Wait! I just want to meet my father."

The woman stared, mouth agape, color leeching from her face. When she finally spoke, he could barely hear her. "Your *father?* What on earth are you talking about?"

He took a half step forward, silently pleading for her help. "There's no easy way to say this. I have reason to believe your husband is my father." He hesitated, trying to keep the longing from his voice. "I, uh, want to meet him."

"There must be some mistake—"

"No, ma'am, I don't think so. Did your husband serve in the Vietnam War in 1968?"

Mutely, she nodded, her hands locked on the door.

Gently he continued. "He knew my mother there."

The woman raked her eyes over him as if assessing his resemblance to her husband. Time stood still. Only the cries of mountain jays broke the silence.

At last, with tears pooling in her eyes, she whispered, "Come inside."

CHAPTER ONE

I THOUGHT MARK TAYLOR would never leave. Now I'm pacing from room to room, disbelief lodged in my chest. Never once with Sam has there been a whisper of another woman. Yet in this young man's tall, well-built frame, the way he tilts his head when listening and the matchless blue of his eyes, I see my husband. Everything in me screams denial, but the truth is hard to escape. Even if Sam was ignorant of the pregnancy, as Mark claims, did he think this chapter of his life could remain forever closed?

Oddly, despite my anger and hurt, I found it impossible to ignore the entreaty in Mark Taylor's voice or to doubt his sincerity. But I know Sam. A sudden confrontation between the two of them would never have worked. Even so, I resent having to be the one to break the news when he returns from Boulder where he's helping our younger daughter Lisa paint her living room.

I've taken Mark Taylor's contact information

and encouraged him to return to Savannah if Sam doesn't phone him at his motel within a couple of days.

Numb, I wander to the picture window overlooking the tarn, now turning steely under gathering clouds. All my certainties are evaporating like a shifting mountain mist. In their place, questions and accusations swirl.

THE NEXT EVENING, I hardly let Sam hang up his jacket before turning on him. "You've been keeping quite the secret all these years. Did you ever plan to tell me or was I just supposed to drift along in ignorance?"

His eyes widen with incomprehension. "Tell you what?"

"About your fling during the Vietnam War. About the total stranger who appeared at the door yesterday announcing himself as your son."

"What in blazes are you talking about?"

With barely controlled fury, I repeat Mark Taylor's claim. About his mother Diane and her gallant sacrifice in not telling Sam she was pregnant. About Mark's stateside birth and his mother's marriage to Rolf Taylor, whose name is on the birth certificate. "He's a grown man now. He wants to meet you."

Sam turns to granite before my eyes. "I have no

knowledge of any baby. I won't see him. He's nothing to me."

I am speechless, appalled by his cold indifference to his son and to my feelings. Finally I choke out, "Was *she* also nothing to you?"

"For God's sake, Isabel!"

"Answer the question."

"Do you think I'd have spent over forty-five years of my life with you if she meant more to me?"

"Well, you certainly spent a bit of time with her. Enough to impregnate her."

"Christ, Izzy, I was lonely and scared."

"Welcome to the waiting wives' club. Do you think it was any picnic being at home and imagining the worst?"

His shoulders slump. "I don't know what to say to you, except I'm sorry. I never wanted you to find out."

"I can believe that. But you should have told me. Then I wouldn't have had to open the door yesterday and get blindsided by Mark Taylor. Who, by the way looks just like you. He wants to meet you. Whether I like it or not, you owe him something."

"Not now." The grandfather clock sounds like a ticking bomb. "I can't deal with this just like that." He snaps his fingers to emphasize the point. "I need time. I have to go away."

"*You* have to go away? What about me? Am I

just supposed to keep the home fires burning, carry on as if my whole life hasn't been turned upside down?"

"Izzy, please understand. I have to think."

"You know what? I don't care what you need right now. This is always the way you handle trouble. You run, Sam, you run. Like a coward."

He takes me by the arms. "Please, I need time."

I hear the coldness in my voice. "And I need an explanation."

He raises his hands in a gesture of helplessness. "I know you do. Believe me, I've regretted the incident ever since. It was nothing. It was wartime and—"

"Save your excuses for another time—after you've had your precious time to think. And whatever happens, Sam, a son is not nothing. Remember that."

I leave the room seething. History repeats itself. Sam crawls into his cave, and all I can do is wait and wonder how I could have been married, happily for the most part, to a man with such a devastating secret.

SAM DEPARTS THE NEXT morning for Montana where his air force buddy Mike has offered his vacation cabin on the Yellowstone River. The fiction is that Sam is on a fishing trip. The truth? He's escaping.

The day after he leaves, our older daughter Jenny comes up from Colorado Springs where she lives with her contractor husband Don. Usually I look forward to her visits. Today, though, the effort to mask my feelings is almost more than I can handle.

"Since Daddy's in Montana, I thought you might like company," Jenny says from the kitchen where she's making our lunch—tuna salad. "Besides, I'm kind of lonely myself, now that both girls are off at Colorado State."

"Empty nest?" I query from the breakfast room where I'm setting the table.

She grins wistfully. "I always thought I'd be immune."

"Impossible," I assure her. "Not if you love your children."

After making small talk during our meal, we retire to the family room, where she settles on the sofa with a book, our tiger cat Orville curled in her lap. I sit in my chair, knitting. Fifteen minutes pass before she lays down her novel. "Have you thought any more about Lisa's and my suggestion that you write your memoirs?"

"I don't know how I could find the hours."

"Mother, you're running out of excuses. Now that Daddy's off fishing, you'll have plenty of time to give it a try."

My forty-five-year-old firstborn is every bit as stubborn now as she was as a toddler when, arms folded defiantly, she would stomp her foot and tell me "no." She wore me down then, and nothing seems to have changed because I'm actually considering doing what she asks.

"My life isn't that exciting."

"Nonsense. Your history is interesting to us. We really don't know that much about what you were like as a girl or about your early married years. It'll be a legacy for your grandchildren."

"I wouldn't know where to start."

Jenny fixes me with her brown eyes, so like mine. "At the beginning, of course."

How can I tell her it isn't the beginning I'm worried about. That part I can handle. But the rest? How honest can I be? Particularly in light of recent events. Our daughters will expect portraits of the parents they think they know.

Jenny reaches into her tote bag. "Here." She thrusts a thick journal into my hands, then pulls out a package of my favorite ballpoint pens and plops it on the table. "Now you have no excuse. What have you got to hide? Just pick up a pen and jump in."

What have you got to hide? My thoughts leap to Mark Taylor. Oh, my darling girl, life isn't always as it appears. Dreams become distorted, we do things we never thought we would, and in the twinkling of an eye everything changes.

Jenny arches an eyebrow and waits for my answer.

I sigh. "You're not letting me wiggle out of this, are you?"

Her mouth twitches in a mischievous smile. "I of the iron will? Of course, not." She sobers. "Please, Mom."

Picking up the journal, I thumb through the blank pages, wondering how I can possibly fill them. Wondering how to keep the truth from shattering my daughters' illusions.

"What if you learn some things you'd rather not know?"

"Ooh…" My daughter shivers with delight. "Family skeletons? I can't wait."

"Don't be too sure."

"Do it for us, please, Mom?"

In my head I fast-forward a film of memories, the laughter and tears of a lifetime welling within me. I nod. "I'll try."

After Jenny leaves, I move to the window with its view of the mountains, now in early autumn adorned with skirts of golden aspen. So many years. So many subjects I'd sooner avoid. But I cannot write a fairy tale, especially not now, when the happily-ever-after is in doubt. Sitting in the armchair that has been my refuge for years, I pick up a pen and open the journal. Where to start?

Glancing around the room, my focus settles first on the man-size sofa and recliner, then on the stone fireplace and finally on the floor-to-ceiling bookcase. As if drawn by a magnet, my eyes light on the small figurine peering at me from the fourth shelf. The Buddha-shaped body is both grotesque and comical, but it is the impish, all-knowing smile that pierces my heart. The billiken.

Now I know how to begin.

Springbranch, Louisiana
1945

THE PEALING CHURCH BELLS and deafening staccato of firecrackers mark the event forever in my memory. My scholarly father scooped me into his arms and danced me up and down the sidewalk among throngs of neighbors spilling from their houses. "The Japanese have surrendered," he shouted. "Praise the Lord, the war is over!" Then cradling me close, he whispered for my ear alone. "Remember this day always, Isabel. Freedom has prevailed."

I didn't know what *prevailed* meant, but I understood something momentous had happened.

I can still picture the tear-stained face of Mrs. Ledoux, whose son was on a ship somewhere in the Pacific, and hear the pop of the champagne cork from Old Man Culpepper's front porch. Small boys beat tattoos on improvised drums and grown men waved flags semaphore-style over their heads.

I was six and had no memory of a time before rationing, savings stamps and victory gardens. When the family gathered around the radio listening to news from the front, even though I couldn't grasp much, I knew "our boys" were heroes. But the freedom my daddy talked about was a puzzling concept. Looking back, I realize how far from harm's way we were in the small, backwater town in north central Louisiana.

That night Grandmama Phillips, my mother's mother, led me into her upstairs bedroom. After Grandpapa died, she came to live with us and brought an astonishing array of antique furniture, including a china closet, a Victrola, two rockers and a canopy bed. Her room was an exotic sanctuary for me, smelling of Evening in Paris cologne, peppermint drops and patchouli incense.

Sleepy after the V-J Day celebration, I crawled onto my grandmother's lap and nestled against her bosom. "*Ma petite* Isabel, this is a joyous end to long, troubling years. I have something special to give you to remember this day. A token to remind you how every once in a while, things turn out exactly as they should."

Reaching into the pocket of her flowered smock, she brought forth the odd-looking figurine that I'd seen sitting in the china cabinet among her collection of delicate teacups and saucers. Smiling beatifically, as if giving me a gift of great worth, Grandmama placed the grayish statuette in my small, cupped hands. The contours of the Buddha-esque body felt cool and soothing, and I giggled when I gazed at the face, bearing an elfin grin as if he and I shared a delicious secret. "What is it, Grandmama?"

"A billiken. My father brought this to me in 1909 after a trip to Missouri." She ran a finger over the billiken's head. "He's an extraordinary little god." Then, taking him from me, she upended him. On the bottom was a circular brass plaque with an inscription around the circumference. "Can you read this, Bel?"

I screwed up my face and studied the words. She took over for me. "'The god of things as they ought to be.'" She chuckled. "No wonder he's smiling, *ma chère.* Today is one of those rare times when things are, indeed, exactly as they ought to be."

I fell asleep clutching the billiken, secure in the knowledge that I was safe, the world was at peace and things truly were as God intended.

LET ME TELL YOU more about my family. I was an only child, doted upon by the three adults in the home. Sometimes I wonder if their attention to me wasn't, in part, a means of buffering themselves from one another.

Daddy was a short, chubby man who wore thick glasses and taught English literature at the local college. In a household of females, his study was his haven, and he retreated there most evenings to prepare lessons or grade papers. My mother deferred to him, but with ill-concealed martyrdom, as if she were silently screaming, "I made my bed, and now I *will* lie in it."

Grandmama, ever the romantic, amused herself by listening to radio soap operas. When I stayed home from school sick, she would bring me into her bedroom where we would snuggle under her comforter, breathless for the latest adventures of Helen Trent or "Our Gal Sunday." My grandmother admired swashbuckling rogues of the Rhett Butler mold. Occasionally she would mutter things like, "Your daddy just needs to stand his ground with Renie" or, referring to one of the soap opera idols, "Now, there's a man for you—he's out in the world doing something." Young as I was, I knew what had been left unsaid. "Unlike your father."

In retrospect, I see she was preparing me for my own Clark Gable, spinning romantic notions of the day my personal knight in shining armor would appear.

I loved Grandmama dearly, but I wished she saw in Daddy what I did—a courtly and gentle man who made me his intellectual companion and in whose eyes I could do no wrong. And what of his interior life? Did he regret marrying my mother, or, in his own way, did he care for her? Had he ever harbored other—different—aspirations? Amazingly, I never heard him utter regrets or say an unkind word about either Mother or Grandmama.

Irene Phillips Ashmore. My mother. It's hard, even now, to imagine she was Grandmama's daughter. There wasn't a romantic bone in her body. Businesslike, practical and fixated on propriety, she was the engine that kept the household machine running smoothly.

She found fulfillment in the Women's Club of Springbranch. No one ever worked harder to be accepted in society, or what passed for it in our community, than my mother.

And who was expected to be the living embodiment of her social ambitions? Her daughter. Me. Isabel Irene Ashmore.

Springbranch, Louisiana
Early 1950s

POSTWAR SPRINGBRANCH WAS a place of promise. A development of starter ranch homes sprouted in the field beyond the water tower, new model automobiles replaced prewar coupes and sedans, and enrollment at the college reflected the popularity of the G.I. Bill.

My mother's postwar efforts were directed toward transforming her gangly adolescent daughter into a lady. Not just any lady, mind you, but a genteel Southern lady. Posture: "Isabel Irene Ashmore, stand up straight." Etiquette: "I didn't hear you say *ma'am*." Table manners: "My dear, a lady never talks with her mouth full."

I dreaded most her advice concerning boys, whom she referred to as *beaux*. "Flirt, Isabel. Bat those pretty brown eyes." I had little interest in the pimply-faced males in my class at Springbranch Elementary School. The idea of flirting with them was humiliating.

Mother meant well, but I always believed I fell short of her expectations. Even though she is long dead, I don't remember ever experiencing unconditional love from her. Maybe she had to be the way she was. Daddy was lost in his books and Grandmama filled my head with fairy tales. Somebody had to take me in hand.

Throughout my girlhood, I did my best to please her. Every Sunday I wore a hat and gloves to St. John's Episcopal Church. I didn't use slang expressions, and I always changed out of my school dress before going outside to play. I even practiced the piano the requisite half hour a day.

Not surprisingly, I liked school—the wooden desks lined up in neat rows, the dulcet tones of teachers' voices, the sense of accomplishment in winning a spelling bee. I tried very hard to be what others referred to as "a good girl."

In sixth grade Twink came into my life. School started right after Labor Day and standing just inside Miss Vinnie's classroom was a strange girl, covered with freckles and sporting a wild mop of carrot-colored curls. Never had I seen such green eyes. She was a leprechaun come to life, and I loved her from that first moment.

"Hi." She took a step forward. "This is my first day."

"I know," I said. "What's your name?"

"Twink Montgomery."

"Twink?"

She scowled, daring me to laugh. "Aurelia Mae Starr Montgomery. How would you like it if people called you Aurelia Mae?" She strung out each syllable in challenge.

"I wouldn't, I guess." In fact, I wasn't crazy about my mother calling me Isabel Irene. From that first meeting with Twink, I longed for a nickname. "I'm Isabel Ashmore."

"Isabel." She rolled the name around on her tongue. "That's not as bad as Aurelia. Close, though."

We burst into a fit of giggles, the first of many.

When I told Mother about my new friend, she was horrified. "Twink? What kind of name is that? What are her people thinking? Why, why—" she sputtered "—it's almost as bad as someone referring to you as Izzy!"

Izzy. Now there was a nickname! From the beginning, I liked it, but I knew Mother would swoon if she ever heard anybody call me that. Twink often used it when we were alone, but was careful not to slip in front of Mother.

Something weird happened the next year. Boys started paying attention to Twink and me. Not in a smooth-talking, Tab Hunter manner, but awkwardly, fumblingly.

Then, over the summer, to my horror, my breasts started budding. Mother and Grandmama simpered about how wonderful it was that I was "developing." I hated that word. It conjured images of being sent, like a roll of film, to the Kodak camera shop for some mysterious metamorphosis.

Those times seem pretty tame now. As a naive thirteen-year-old I had never heard of condoms, wet dreams or oral sex. My goodness, finding out about menstruation had about done me in.

Oh, I started to write about Twink and me. She was still straight as a stick, but didn't have any qualms when it came to talking to boys, whereas I became virtually tongue-tied.

This brings me to the Springbranch Cotillion—a tradition as established as sweetened ice tea. Held in the parish hall of the Episcopal church and sponsored by the Springbranch Women's Club, the Cotillion was a series of ballroom dancing classes for eighth graders from the "best" families.

Every other Tuesday evening, dressed in our taffeta dresses and black ballet slippers, we girls were dropped off at the church where we suffered under the tutelage of Mrs. Collins Wentworth, self-proclaimed grande dame of local society.

Our very first night, Twink sailed toward the boys, dragging me reluctantly in her wake. Dressed in ill-fitting suits, shirts and even bow ties, they looked nothing like they did at school. When the boys averted their eyes and shuffled their feet, I realized they were no more enthusiastic than I was about the upcoming ordeal.

Mrs. Wentworth, clapping her hands over her head, sashayed to the center of the floor. "Please number off for partners." My eleven was matched by Laidslaw Grosbeak's. Yes, that was actually his name, and it suited him, because his thin, sallow face was overwhelmed by a long, aquiline nose.

I towered over him. In memory, I can still smell the combination of his Juicy Fruit gum and Brylcreem hair tonic.

Twink shot a triumphant smile over Jimmy Comstock's back. With the luck of the Irish, she had snagged the man of our dreams. After the briefest instruction, they were actually waltzing, while Laidslaw and I were still stumping in one place, eyes fixed on our uncooperative feet.

The Grand March mercifully brought an end to the evening. Two by two and then four by four, we circled the room and then were dismissed into the humid Louisiana night.

"How was the dance?" Grandmama asked later, her eyes sparkling in giddy anticipation. I stood in the living room doorway, mute with embarrassment.

Mother looked up from her darning. "I'm sure she enjoyed it, Mama." She turned to me. "Didn't you, Isabel?"

"It was all right." I started toward my bedroom, eager to strip off the scratchy dress and remove the glittery rhinestone barrettes from my hair.

"Tell us more. Who did you dance with?" Hearing my grandmother's plaintive tone, I knew a debriefing was unavoidable. Surrendering, I sat beside her and did my inventive best to paint a glowing picture of the debacle.

When I finished, Mother, a triumphant gleam in her eye, said, "See, Mama, I told you Isabel would do us proud."

That night as I lay in my bed watching the moon rise over the treetops and feeling the restless breeze cool my body, I had the strongest premonition that something important was expected of me. Something involving boys.

Shortly before I closed my eyes, a shaft of moonlight settled on the billiken sitting on my curio shelf. For the fraction of a second, he seemed to wink at me.

EVEN THOUGH TWINK'S parents had bought an antebellum Southern mansion and drove the latest model cars, they were carpetbaggers in Springbranchian eyes. Mr. Montgomery had made his money in stocks, a specious enterprise in our part of the agricultural South. Mrs. Montgomery, called "Honey," defied convention by hosting cocktail brunches on Sunday and driving to Shreveport to have her hair done.

I reveled in the sense of the forbidden whenever I was in their home, where full liquor decanters and a silver cigarette box sat on a table right in the living room. If my mother had known, she might have forbidden me to be friends with Twink.

Best of all was the gazebo at the back of the Montgomerys' deep yard. Shaded from view by hundred-year-old oaks, it was our secret hide-away. One hot July afternoon following our eighth grade year, we took lemonades and a Monopoly set out there. But before we set up the board, Twink looked around, making sure she wasn't being observed, and then pulled a soft-covered book from beneath her sleeveless camp shirt. "Want to see what I found?" In her expression excitement mingled with disgust.

Prickles traveled down my spine. "What?" I pulled my legs under me and waited.

"This was in my mother's dresser drawer, way in the back underneath her nightgowns." As if it were a hot potato, she handed me the slim volume.

I had intended to ask why she'd been snooping in her mother's bedroom, but I couldn't. Not after reading the shocking title. *Sexual Secrets of Happy Marriages.*

"Open it." Twink's voice sounded tinny.

I gripped the book between my fingers, sensing I was on the brink of a fateful decision.

"Go ahead, Izzy."

Twink's use of the special nickname commit-ted me in a way nothing else could have. "Okay." I turned to the middle of the book, then blinked, certain I could not be seeing what was there on the page in black and white. "Twink?" Light-headed, I held out the book for her inspection. "Are they doing what I think they are?"

"Yes."

Incredulous, I studied the photograph of the naked couple. I knew vaguely about sperm and eggs and ovulation, but no one, not my mother and not the health teacher, had ever explained in detail about the sex act.

"See—" Twink pointed to the picture "—the man puts his thing in her. Listen here." Turning the page, she read me a graphic account of the mechanics, then flipped to photos of other contorted positions.

"Twink, this is revolting."

"It's icky to think about our parents doing this, isn't it?" she said in a hushed voice.

"*My* parents!" It's a wonder the neighbors didn't hear my shriek of outrage, but the mental image of Irene and Robert Ashmore coupling was utterly incomprehensible.

Twink and I never opened the Monopoly set. Instead we spent the afternoon devouring every lurid detail, alternately horrified and titillated.

Only later, walking home, did the full import hit me. Husbands and wives did this. That's how babies were made. I would someday have to do that thing myself. I remember leaning against the trunk of a tree, on the verge of being sick, trying to catch my breath.

Then another thought came. Grandmama and Mother kept asking me whether I had any beaux. But if they knew what men and women did…

In bed that night, I thought about Laidslaw Grosbeak and Jimmy Comstock. Even Tab Hunter. Then I made a solemn promise to myself. I would die an old maid before I would ever do *that*.

One afternoon with "the book" had shattered the idealized image of Southern womanhood for me. However, all that knowledge couldn't prepare me for what was to come, and before too long, I discovered life always has the capacity to blindside us.

ARMED WITH THE back-to-school issue of *Seventeen,* Twink and I assembled our wardrobe for the most momentous step in our lives—high school. The three-story brick building, two blocks off the town square, had not yet been remodeled. Tall, heavy-sash windows opened to whatever breeze might come, desks rested on polished wooden floors and freshly cleaned blackboards bordered the rooms. But to Twink and me it was Valhalla— the place where the gods and goddesses of our adolescence resided.

On that first day, although I had mastered my

locker combination, I was fearful about getting lost. What if I was late for a class? To add to my insecurities, I caught sight of the head cheerleader, the varsity quarterback and the senior class president, whose green eyes and dimples made me weak in the knees. I had never felt so out of place or awkward.

But that changed when I walked into algebra and saw Taylor Jennings. He had the dark good looks of a Creole grandee and a sultry voice that transported me to moonlit bayous. Sitting at my desk, feeling his gaze on me, the hairs on the nape of my neck stirred. In the pit of my stomach were funny, unfamiliar sensations. Unbidden, the photos in "the book" rose in my memory, and I felt myself blush.

Walking home with Twink, I mentioned Taylor.

"He's handsome, all right," she agreed. "If you like freshmen." She smirked, then did a jig step. "I'm setting my sights on Jay Owensby."

I stopped dead in my tracks. "He's a *junior.*"

She giggled. "So? I've always adored older men."

"Aurelia Mae Starr Montgomery, are you keeping secrets?"

"I was going to tell you. Dad hired Jay two weeks ago to mow our lawn. You should see him without a shirt." She made a play of fanning herself. "Anyway, we've been talking, and last night he came over to pick up his check. One thing led to another and…"

I wanted to shake her. "What do you mean?"

"He asked me to go for a walk and we ended up in the park." Her eyes twinkled mischievously. "Oh, Izzy, it was di-vine!"

"What was?"

"The kiss."

She said it so matter-of-factly, I wasn't sure I'd heard correctly. "The *kiss?*"

"Believe me, it was nothing like those stupid games of post office." She shivered with delight. "I can't wait for the next one."

I wanted details, but at the same time I felt like a novice in the presence of the initiated. "Are you two, like, dating?"

"He's taking me to the football game this weekend. He has a car. Who knows? We may end up at the lake for a smooch."

"A smooch?"

She put an arm around my shoulder and leaned closer. "And maybe more."

"More?" In my bewilderment, I couldn't stop parroting her.

"Oh, Isabel, it's all starting—just like in the movies. I'm so glad we're growing up."

By the time we reached the corner where we

parted ways, we had changed the subject, yet all I could think of was the change in Twink.

DESPITE TYPICAL TEENAGE trials, high school was an idyllic interlude. I enjoyed my classes and, committed as I was to pleasing my parents, Daddy in particular, I excelled. That achievement was not without its price, however. I soon discovered that boys were not interested in the quality of my mind.

I dated some, but usually other serious students, whose claim to fame lay not on the football field but in labs and at debate tournaments. Like most teens, I fantasized about being the homecoming queen, escorted to the prom by a handsome, champion athlete. Instead, my date was the aforementioned Laidslaw Grosbeak, who, at least, had grown ten inches and adopted his middle name, Barton. And yes, Twink *was* the queen.

As far as what passed for romance was concerned, I lived vicariously through Twink, who knew how to flirt, lead a boy just to the point of no return, cast him aside and mysteriously remain on good terms with him. She also gave me my first view of the world beyond Springbranch. At least twice a year her family vacationed in exotic spots like New York City, London and Honolulu, scenes I could only imagine from magazines or television. Much as I wanted to see such places for myself, I was intimidated by the unfamiliar. I couldn't envision a future that didn't include Springbranch, a provincial outlook that hardly prepared me for what happened later.

One snapshot from those years summarizes the two of us. We stand in caps and gowns, arms entwined. Mortarboard at a rakish angle, Twink grins triumphantly at the camera, while I face straight ahead, my mortarboard aligned in a scholarly manner, clutching my diploma protectively. "Graduation is only the beginning," she appears to announce, whereas my demeanor screams a need to remain eternally at Springbranch High School.

How often I have appreciated Twink's adventurous spirit. Even considering her two divorces and years of caring for her ailing mother, she has rarely lost her optimism. I, on the other hand, am full of reservations and second thoughts, which makes this trip down memory lane both necessary and bittersweet.

CHAPTER TWO

Springbranch, Louisiana
August, 1957

TWINK AND I WERE TOGETHER every day of what was to be our last Springbranch summer. In mid-August Twink's parents abruptly put their house on the market under suspicious circumstances. Twink acted unfazed. "After all," she said with a toss of her head, "I'll be back East at college. What do I care where they live?"

But she did care. A great deal. She'd told me once that Springbranch was the only place her family had lived for more than two years. The town represented roots, and poignantly, so did my family and I.

Not that Mother ever fully accepted Twink's eccentricities, but Grandmama relished another rapt listener for her stories, and Daddy enjoyed it when we girls sprawled on the Oriental rug in his study and read while he worked.

Although Twink may have appeared undaunted

by change, I couldn't even pretend to be unaffected. We were attending different colleges—she, a prestigious women's college and I, the state university on an academic scholarship. Knowing we'd be apart even during vacations made this transition all the more unsettling. The last night before Twink left for school, Mother allowed me to sleep over at the Montgomerys' house.

Twink's belongings had been boxed up, ready for the family's move to Baltimore, and open suitcases awaited last-minute additions. Her stripped room was symbolic of change. Gentle breezes stirred the ruffled curtains at the window, and our voices echoed off the bare walls. Twink seemed determined to get through the night without sadness, but I barely held myself together. Determinedly cheerful, she recalled our meeting, high school escapades and secret crushes. It was after two when we finally turned out the light. I lay in the twin bed, staring at the leafy branches of the huge oak outside the window, choking back my pain and loss and wondering when I would ever see my friend again.

Just as I was about to drift off, Twink spoke. "Are you awake?"

"Yes."

"You'll be all right, you know."

It was as if she'd read my mind, knew how apprehensive I was about going to Louisiana State

University and understood how much I was going to miss her friendship. A lone tear trickled down my cheek. "It won't be the same without you."

"I know." I detected a hitch in her voice. "Here's the thing, Izzy. Things can't always stay the same, even if we'd like them to. Look at it this way. We're ready for new adventures in that wonderful world out there."

That alien world terrified me. Yet in that moment I found myself wanting to comfort Twink, whose voice betrayed her bravado. Oddly, that made me feel better. I wasn't the only one uncertain about the future.

"A whole new world…but, Twink, I can't do this unless I know we'll always be friends, no matter what."

"Till we die," she whispered.

I echoed her words. "Till we die."

We were such innocents, little dreaming what changes and upheavals life would bring. But we understood the solemnity of our pledge, and we honor it still.

Baton Rouge
1957-1958

COLLEGE. THE HALCYON years between adolescence and adulthood. Or so they say. First semester of my freshman year, from the frenzy of sorority rush to the rigor of final exams, I felt overwhelmed. So many people. Unfamiliar surroundings. Sharing a room for the first time. And the crushing weight of my mother's expectations.

Before I left for the university, I'd been unaware that a coed's true purpose in attending college was snagging a husband. But in Mother's weekly phone calls, she made that abundantly clear. "Have you met anyone yet?" *Anyone,* of course, was code for Mr. Right. I *was* meeting some college men at fraternity mixers, but they weren't lining up to escort me to parties.

Gradually, I settled into a niche. I enjoyed sorority life, and once or twice a month one of my sisters arranged a blind date for me, but none of them progressed beyond friendship. Women today have choices, but back then, college, for most, was a marital hunting ground. We gave lip service to majoring in education, nursing or home economics, but few of us expected to be employed beyond our first pregnancy.

Meanwhile, Twink regaled me in letters and phone calls with accounts of wild house parties, weekends in New York City and the "divine" men she was meeting. I wasn't exactly jealous because I knew such glamorous experiences weren't for me, and yet....

My sophomore year was easier. Living in the sorority house gave me a comforting sense of home, I knew my place and began to understand the usefulness of my English lit studies. Yet I was no closer to satisfying my mother's ambitions. The fact of the matter was that I was in no hurry. Marriage was a distant goal. College men either terrified me with their drinking exploits and masculine swagger or bored me with their immaturity.

Throughout my first two years at LSU, the billiken sat on the dresser in my cubbyhole of a room, mocking me with its silence.

Baton Rouge
1959-60

HONESTLY, I'D EXPECTED my college experience to be like the glossy color photos in the school catalog, where I'd be happily waving a purple and gold pennant in the student cheering section or strolling hand-in-hand with a handsome fellow sporting a letter jacket.

Amazingly, in my junior year that's exactly what happened. Drew Mayfield came into my life. If Mother had ordered him from a husband catalog, he couldn't have more neatly fit her mold. His résumé was impeccable: honor student, captain of the golf team, treasurer of the top fraternity, a pre-law major. From Mother's viewpoint his most important credential lay in the fact his father was a federal judge.

Drew was handsome and innately kind. All Southern gentlemen model courtesy, but many practice it in chauvinistic, self-aggrandizing ways. Not Drew. He treated me like a lady, even a cherished one. Therein lay the problem. He was perfect…on paper. We walked hand-in-hand down azalea-lined sidewalks, he bought me a chrysanthemum corsage for homecoming and nominated me for sweetheart of his fraternity. We became a couple. At the end of that year, beneath a full Southern moon, he gave me his fraternity pin.

When I went home for the summer, Mother was ecstatic. For once, I was convinced I'd pleased her. She pored over photographs of Drew and me, and couldn't hear enough about our courtship. Yet the more I repeated the story, the more removed I felt, as if I were observing a film entitled the *The Good Daughter.*

Drew drove up from New Orleans twice that summer and succeeded in charming my mother and grandmother. Daddy was his usual chivalrous but inscrutable self. Drew seemed maddeningly at home in Springbranch. I say maddeningly, because I caught myself trying to discover a flaw in him. Surely he would be out of place in our small town. But he wasn't. Even Eunice Culpepper, our nosy neighbor, fell under his spell.

I liked him. I really did. And I'm reasonably certain he believed himself in love with me. By the beginning of our senior year, we had a tacit understanding that we would marry following graduation. Mother was already considering the guest list and the seasonal flowers that would adorn the church. I was swept away in a tidal wave of others' expectations.

It took Twink to ask the question. "Do you love him so madly your body quakes with excitement?"

I clenched the phone and swallowed the lump in my throat.

"Izzy?" The compassion in my friend's voice undid me.

"I...uh, I..."

"The answer's no, isn't it?"

How desperately I wanted to tell Twink that Drew was the most exciting man in the world, that he did, indeed, make me limp with desire. That all the pictures in the book we had read in that gazebo years ago had taken on glorious new meaning.

You might logically assume I broke off with Drew. But I didn't. He was safe. Predictable. I liked him. Best of all, he pleased my mother. I could learn to love him, I told myself. We could have a nice life together.

Oh, what a weak word "nice" is.

Springbranch
1960

IN EARLY NOVEMBER OF that year, I was called home from school. Grandmama, who had grown increasingly frail, was in the hospital. Seeing her pale, shrunken body on the bed, I faced mortality for the first time. When I picked up her hand, the paperlike, wrinkled skin felt warm, but her breath came in labored gasps. Her white hair, usually perfectly coiffed, hung lankly. Nurses came and went, but I felt compelled to stay. From the hall I heard whispered consultations. *Congestive heart failure. Not long now.* Words that pierced my soul.

Daddy sat in the waiting room, a volume of Wordsworth his only company. Mother bustled. Straightening pillows. Filling the water carafe. Adjusting the blinds.

But I sat, willing each new inhalation and realizing how much I loved Grandmama and depended on her. I had never had to work to please her. Even if I'd told her the truth years ago about the cotillion disaster, she would have hugged me and said, "There, there, Bel."

Later that night after Mother left the room, I found myself humming "I'll Fly Away" and blinking back tears. Then I felt Grandmama's thumb caressing the back of my hand. When I looked up, her eyes were open, her mouth curved in the trace of a smile. "Bel," she murmured.

"I'm here."

With surprising strength, she drew me closer. I leaned over the bed. "That boy," she whispered.

"Drew?"

She nodded. "Passion." The word had the force of an imperative.

I had no answer.

Then came the last words I ever heard my grandmother utter. "Things as they ought to be, *ma petite.*"

Then she closed her eyes, gave a long sigh and left me.

Baton Rouge
1961

EVEN THOUGH I KNEW in my heart I was betraying both myself and Grandmama, I agreed to marry Drew. Of all the men I had met at college, he was by far the best match. We had much in common. Our families approved. We discussed names for the two children we intended to have. Besides, marriage was the "done" thing. With few exceptions, my sorority sisters either were already married or in the throes of planning their weddings.

Drew's kisses didn't send me to the moon, but they were pleasant enough. Heavy petting, while arousing, seemed a bit clinical, but so had the photographs in *the* book. Back then, though, I didn't know anything different.

St. John's was reserved for September 8, the women's auxiliary scheduled to cater the reception and the Springbranch Country Club booked for the rehearsal dinner. Twink was to be my maid of honor. Mother was in her element. Things were proceeding precisely according to her plan. Daddy spent even more time in his study.

I don't know if it was born out of a subconscious need for self-preservation or a desire to escape, but I asked my parents for only one thing for a college graduation present. A trip to Atlanta, where the Montgomerys were living, to visit Twink, before plunging into final bridal preparations.

And that, as they say, made all the difference.

Atlanta, Georgia
Summer 1961

TWINK MET ME AT the Atlanta terminal, her smile as infectious as always, her freckles giving her a Doris Day insouciance. We shrieked, we hugged, we jumped up and down and then repeated the process. She loaded my bags into a Lincoln Continental convertible and swooped out of the parking lot, red curls lifting in the breeze. Above

the roar of wind and traffic, she pointed out land-
marks. Finally we entered an old neighborhood of
lovely Southern and Greek Revival homes, with
well-tended formal gardens shaded by century-
old trees. "Pretty impressive, huh?" She winked.
"Wait until you see Tara."

She slowed, pulling through wrought-iron
gates, and we began a gradual climb, past a fish
pond, a gazebo and a caretaker's home. At the
crest of the hill, I saw it—the massive three-story
white house with Greek columns. Twink stopped
the car and leaned back, arms folded across her
chest. "The parents are on the upswing again."

An understatement, particularly by Springbranch
standards. Speechless, I realized I was far out of my
element. My thoughts flew to the clothes I had
packed—store-bought, gauche. Before I could
focus on my discomfort, Twink leaped from the car,
grabbed my suitcase and put her arm around me.
Leaning close, she said, "It's just me, Izzy. You'll
be fine. All you have to do is pretend you're in a
movie." Once again she'd read my mind.

Later that night, settled on the four-poster in her
spacious bedroom, decorated in a pink-and-white
magnolia motif, we shared the six-pack of beer
she'd liberated from the restaurant-sized kitchen.
"Okay," she commenced. "I want to hear every-

thing about Drew, and please tell me you're not choosing fussy organdy bridesmaid dresses."

She didn't immediately probe my carefully suppressed reservations, but shocked me by the question she asked after I'd waxed eloquent about Drew's stellar qualities. "Is he good in bed?"

"Twink!" The sultry Southern night echoed my dismay.

She threw herself dramatically across the bed. "Isabel Irene, surely you're not marrying before trying him out."

My fire-engine red face gave me away.

"Oh, God." She sat up and took both my hands in hers. "Honey, it's no big deal." She smiled impishly. "Mostly it's a lot of fun."

My stomach soured. "You mean, you've done it?"

"Me and most of your lah-de-dah sorority sisters."

"You think?" I couldn't process the images bombarding my brain.

"Is it Drew? You don't think he's...?" She waggled her fingers back and forth in a this-way, that-way fashion.

I was horrified. "What a thing to say! And no, I'm sure he's not."

"Well, my advice, sugar, is to try the merchandise before buying."

Deep in the pit of my stomach, I knew she was

right. I wanted fireworks and shooting stars. I'd experienced none with Drew. Before Twink's question, I'd successfully buried my doubts, but her honesty forced them to the surface.

Sensing my discomfort, she reached for the church key and opened another beer, thrusting it into my hands. "Drink up. You don't have to decide anything this very minute. Anyway, I want to tell you about the garden party we're throwing in your honor tomorrow night, not to mention the country club dance on Saturday. We're going to have so much fun." She flopped over onto her stomach. "You will not believe the dreamy men in this town. Why, chile, I just flit from one to another like a bee sippin' honey." Her low laugh had a distinctly seductive sound.

I studied the diamond on my ring finger, incapable of imagining how she handled multiple suitors. I took a swig of beer, suddenly missing Drew. All this talk of sex, parties and glamorous men made me long for the mundane, the dull, the safe. For my fiancé.

I REMEMBER THE MOMENT as if it happened yesterday. There is no way I can adequately describe the impact. Let me set the scene.

Chinese lanterns strung from tree to tree illuminated the flagstone patio leading to the

Olympic-size pool in which colorful blossoms floated. A white tent stretched over the manicured lawn; inside, a quintet played romantic dance music. Jacketed waiters manned the buffet table and fully stocked bar. Our hostess, Honey Montgomery, was stunning in a silver-lamé evening gown. Mr. Montgomery, a cigar in one hand, mingled with groups of tuxedo-clad gentlemen. Twink had given me good advice when she told me to pretend I was in a movie. I fully expected Elizabeth Taylor to make a grand entrance. Twink had been accurate about the young men of Atlanta—tall, well-groomed, mannerly and utterly gorgeous in their white dinner jackets. Not to mention a trio of handsome young lieutenants from Bainbridge Air Force Base.

To my utter horror, before we sat down for dinner, Honey stepped to the top of the stairs leading to the pool, signaled for quiet and introduced little ole me from Springbranch, Louisiana, to the assembled partygoers. Clutching the skirt of my pale blue chiffon gown, I felt frumpy and exposed.

As soon after dinner as I could politely excuse myself, I escaped to the seclusion of a garden bench nestled in a bower of roses beyond the tent. I knew I couldn't remain cowering there, but I needed to gather myself. I had always known that

Twink's world was vastly different from my own. I just hadn't realized how different. She took the opulence and sophistication in stride. I was totally intimidated, a pond fish washed up on a tropical beach. I had no idea how I would endure the rest of the evening.

Wallowing in my social ineptitude, I didn't hear him approach. I only know that when I raised my head, the handsomest young man I had ever seen was standing over me, hands in the pockets of his air force dress uniform pants. His head was slightly cocked to one side, a mischievous grin played on his lips, and he was studying me with the deepest cobalt-blue eyes I had ever seen. My heart stopped. I *was* in a movie.

"Running away?" His voice was like warm brandy. He didn't wait for my answer. "Mind if I join you?"

"A-are you sure?" I stammered.

"Never surer of anything in my life," he said, sitting beside me. "I've been looking for you."

"For me?" The words came out as a squeak.

"I haven't been able to keep my eyes off you all evening."

My breath caught. I couldn't have written a better script myself. "Me?" I was speechless.

He slipped an arm around my bare shoulder

and turned me toward him. "What I'd really like to do is kiss you."

And he did. No fireworks or starbursts in the world could match the thrill and power of that kiss. When we broke apart, he framed my face, brushed one finger across my cheek and with a lazy smile added, "And now I'm going to do it again."

It never occurred to me to deny him. I was helpless, but in some small part of my brain I understood that, until that moment, I had known nothing of the kind of love a man and woman are born to share.

He pulled me to my feet. "Isabel Ashmore." His mouth caressed the words. "Izzy. I'm Sam Lambert and, if you don't mind, I'm claiming you for the rest of the evening."

Mind? I couldn't believe this was happening to me. Yet everything—the night sky, the distant strains of "Deep Purple," the fragrance of roses— whispered, *Do this thing.*

"Why did you call me Izzy?"

He held my hands firmly. "Isabel sounds formal, public. I want our private name. It sounds good, don't you think? Sam and Izzy. Izzy and Sam."

I couldn't help smiling. "Aren't you being a wee bit presumptuous?"

He circled my waist as we strolled up the path toward the tent. "Not at all. I've been waiting for you all my life. When you were introduced this evening, I knew I had to get to know you. I'll be damned if I'll let you get away."

With a sinking sensation, I realized that with my thumb I was fingering my engagement ring. I needed to tell him. To put an end to whatever this was. But at that moment he stopped walking and tilted my chin so that I was looking straight into those sexy eyes, so full of promise. "Tell me you feel it, too."

Grandmama's advice came flooding back to me. *Passion.* Right then I understood that I was caught up in something beyond my control. "I do," I whispered, "and it's scary."

"And wonderful."

"And wonderful."

I know this all sounds corny and clichéd, even melodramatic. But it happened just like that. In an instant, the planets halted in their orbit and my heart knew love.

For the rest of that evening and the days and nights that followed, Sam and I were inseparable. I'm not proud to say it, but I took off my engagement ring and stored it in my jewelry case. Twink gloated like an approving mother cat.

Because Sam was on a weekend pass from the air base where he was stationed for pilot training, time took on urgency. We lounged by the pool, soaking up the sun, oblivious to anyone else. We enjoyed a lopsided game of tennis and left the country club dance Saturday night to lie on a blanket near the eighteenth green, sharing hot kisses in the glimmering, magical moonlight. It was an awakening for me. I had not known my body could quiver with need or that instinct could drive me to abandon.

And we talked. And talked. I had never met anyone who had nurtured an ambition—in his case to be a pilot—and then pursued it with such intensity. A three-sport athlete in high school, he'd been awarded a scholarship to the University of Nebraska, where he'd played varsity basketball and had joined the air force ROTC. When he spoke about his pilot training and his service buddies, his face lit up. This was no boy; this was a man who had embraced his purpose in life. His maturity stirred something deep within me.

Our last night together Sam held me close. "You're my girl. My Southern hothouse flower." He nuzzled my cheek. "My Izzy."

I was besotted. Twink was merciless. "Isabel Irene, you're in love. Why would you settle for anything less? You march right home and cancel that wedding."

"I've had a wonderful time, but, Twink, this isn't reality. It's a fairy tale, and the clock is about to strike midnight. Chances are, I'll never see Sam Lambert again." Even as I said those words, my throat closed in panic.

"Maybe not, but you don't know that. What you do know is that you're not in love with Drew Mayfield. I'm not going to stand by and let you…" she fussed, searching for words "…settle for mediocrity."

It was tempting to follow her advice, but I rationalized that my time with Sam was probably nothing more than one of those heady—but fleeting—summer romances I'd heard other girls talk about. Sure, he'd said he'd call, write. Finally, I decided I'd be a fool to count on anything, given the miles separating us.

Besides, was I willing to scuttle my future because of one gloriously romantic weekend? How could I disappoint Drew? Shatter my mother's hopes? Act so irresponsibly and uncharacteristically?

And yet, how could I not?

CHAPTER THREE

Springbranch, Louisiana

WHEN I RETURNED FROM Atlanta, Mother was knee-deep in wedding preparations, researching fruit-punch recipes and floral arrangements. On her desk were four boxes of invitations: "Dr. and Mrs. Robert James Ashmore request the honor of your presence at the wedding of their daughter Isabel Irene…" I felt sick. But when, at the end of the first week, I hadn't heard from Sam, I wondered if I'd dreamed the encounter or, beyond that, made a complete fool of myself.

"Isabel, can't you demonstrate a little more enthusiasm?" These were Mother's words after we'd spent an afternoon finalizing the guest list. The wedding plans had taken on a life of their own, and I was powerless to stop them, even as I questioned myself. Then two things happened to make the situation worse. I received my first letter from Sam, and Drew arrived for a visit.

In Sam's bold handwriting was a note that was just like him—breezily self-confident with a dash of bravado. And unutterably romantic. I blush even now recalling the pure physicality of my reaction when I tore open the envelope and saw the words *My Izzy*. I soon learned that he, like Twink, could read my mind.

I bet you're wondering about my intentions. If I'm just a guy who came to Atlanta for a weekend to have a good time. Well, I did have a good time, but it's more than that. Izzy, you're the dream I've had for a long time. I'm not going away.

The next day Drew pulled into our driveway and bounded from his car, waving a piece of paper over his head. "I nailed it, Isabel," he said wrapping me in a hug. "The apartment near the law school. This is the lease."

He stood back, awaiting my ecstatic reaction. Furnished apartments near the campus were rare. "That's nice," I murmured, taking the wind out of his sails. The mental picture of us settled on the second floor of a big house surrounded by over-stuffed chairs, tables and, worst of all, a double bed, was overwhelming.

Later that night, Drew and I sat in the porch

swing watching fireflies gather, smelling the musk of the warm night. He had his arm around me. It felt cozy. When he kissed me, I closed my eyes and really tried to experience the spark that would reassure me. Pleasure, familiarity, yes. No spark. He may as well have been the brother I never had.

Meanwhile the letters from Sam continued, much to my mother's disgust. "Isabel, who is this person who keeps writing you? It's not seemly. You're practically a married woman."

She was right. I was defying all the norms of both etiquette and morality. I hated my duplicity. It wasn't fair to Sam and it wasn't fair to Drew. I had to quit playing games.

Two weeks after Drew returned to Baton Rouge, Sam called. "Isabel, there's a man on the phone." My mother's voice dripped disapproval. "He asked for Izzy, for heaven's sake."

I restrained myself from turning cartwheels. Stretching the phone cord around the corner into the dining room hopefully out of Mother's earshot, I answered. "Sam?"

"Hi, darlin'. Are you missing me the way I'm missing you?"

My knees failed me and I crumpled to the floor "Oh, yes."

"That was your mother who answered, I bet. Have you told her about me? About us?"

"Um…"

"I take that as a no. Any particular reason you haven't?"

"It's kind of complicated."

"Complicated as in you're engaged to be married?"

My heart sank. "Did Twink tell you?"

"Yes, thank God. She thinks your wedding would be a mistake. What do you think?"

In that moment I hardly knew my own name. "It's all set, Sam."

"You didn't answer my question. Let me try another. Do you love this guy?"

"Sam, that's not really any of your business."

"Answer the question." The authority in his voice took my breath away.

"He's a wonderful man."

"Listen to yourself, Izzy. I'm a big boy. If you love him, just say so."

I laced the phone cord through my fingers. This was insane. It made no sense to throw over a man like Drew. Not for someone with whom I'd spent less than seventy-two hours. The wedding plans were in the final stages. Drew was the type of man I should marry. Ours would be exactly the kind of life my mother had envisioned for me. "I can't call this marriage off. It's too late."

There was silence on the other end of the line.

Finally, with resignation, Sam repeated the question. "Do you love him?"

"Please, Sam, don't make me say it."

"Make you? Make you? You don't say it because you can't. You love me."

God help me, it was true, but I was paralyzed by indecision. "Sam, please. We have to stop this."

"Damn right, we're going to stop it. I said it before and I'll say it again, I'm not letting you get away. I love you, Izzy. Please say you love me, too."

In answer, I could only whimper.

Within two days Sam had applied for emergency leave. When he arrived on our doorstep, I took one look at him and knew I could never marry Drew. That very evening I packed a small bag, left my parents a note and fled with Sam.

We drove through the night to a town in southern Arkansas where a county judge married us the next morning. Lying in Sam's arms in the lumpy motel bed on our wedding night, I was the happiest, most satisfied woman in the world.

Never mind that I had betrayed Drew, Mother and my Southern upbringing. My father accepted my decision with his usual equanimity, but Mother, furious over my defection and the embarrassment I had caused her, rarely spoke to me until after Jenny was born. As for Drew, when I told him about the elopement, I could have sworn he sounded relieved.

Several weeks later as I packed to join Sam at his new base in Arizona, I tucked the billiken in a corner of my suitcase. "The god of things as they ought to be." My mother had groomed me for one life. But that was her life, not mine. I had chosen another.

Sam Lambert. Grandmama's passion. And the way things ought to be for me.

OUR WHIRLWIND COURTSHIP and rash decision to elope was as out of character for me then as it would be now. It's no secret there was a powerful physical attraction between Sam and me, but that was not sufficient motivation to throw caution to the winds and brave my mother's ire. What was it about the young Sam Lambert that overcame my inhibitions and upbringing?

Quite simply, from the first he seemed to see the real me. To revel in the Izzy he had discovered— and brought to life. For him, I was never typecast as merely a girl who would make an ideal wife, mother and social asset. Somehow he recognized my need to be rescued from convention. To be sure, Grandmama's influence played a role. In the deepest part of myself, I'd always believed in the knight in shining armor. Much as I tried to deny it, I had always known that Drew was not that hero. The magic—and mystery—is that just as Sam recognized me immediately as his Izzy, so I knew, with complete confidence, that he was the man destined for me.

Twink made sure Sam and I had plenty of time to ourselves during that Atlanta weekend. He coaxed from me stories about Springbranch, fascinated by the local customs and mores that had shaped me. Sunday afternoon we lay together in a hammock in the Montgomerys' backyard. He lifted a lock of my hair and grinned that lopsided, charming grin of his. "That Southern belle? She's not you, Izzy," he said.

"Oh, no," I teased. "Then who am I?"

Sobering, he traced a finger down my nose and considered my question. "You are real. Honest, loving and kind. You're a peacemaker. If you had your way, you'd make everybody happy."

"Do I make you happy?" I murmured, my daring surprising me.

"You have no idea," he whispered. Then he leaned forward and kissed me. In that moment the blue sky above faded, the bird calls went silent, and I knew Sam understood me.

"But that's not all," he said, leaning on one elbow looking down at me. "You have an adventurous streak you've never acted on. So tell me, if you were to follow your instincts, what would you do?"

An intense question. One I'd never really considered, but he was right. I spent most of my time and energy concerned with others' expectations. What did I really want? The answer came immediately. I wanted to be with Sam Lambert.

"Enough about me," I said by way of diversion. "How do I know you're not full of cocky flyboy sweet talk? Maybe I'm the most gullible pushover you've come across lately."

"You've seen too many movies. Not all pilots are self-serving bastards."

"Noted," I said. "Change of subject. When did you know you wanted to be a pilot?"

"Ever since I was a kid." His eyes lit up. "The trailer park where we lived was near a small landing strip. I couldn't stay away. One of the mechanics took an interest in me. I grew up with the smells of aviation gas and oil."

"Where was that?"

As Sam sketched more of his background, it became clear we came from two different worlds. He'd grown up in a small town in eastern Colorado where his father worked highway construction. When he was ten, his mother died. As he spoke of her, his jaw tensed, and I could tell how difficult it was for him to share her loss. Then his tone turned bitter. "My father soon found another lover. Jim Beam whiskey."

My throat convulsed as I pictured the mother-less boy emotionally abandoned by his father.

"I was angry. At God. At my mother. And especially at my father. If it hadn't been for Lloyd, I don't know what I'd have done."

"Lloyd?"

"My brother. Four years younger than me. I, uh, kinda took care of him. For sure, nobody else did."

Nothing in my experience had prepared me to imagine a ten-year-old burdened by such adult responsibilities.

"I'm sorry," was the best I could muster.

"Hell." He gathered me close, his blue eyes fastened on mine. "Maybe you're my reward. In that case, it was worth every minute."

Sam had touched my heart in a way I hadn't thought possible. From that moment I understood Grandmama's advice in a whole new way. By passion, she had meant so much more than physical attraction. She'd meant the mysterious, inexplicable connection that binds two people together despite their differences.

There were two Sams I came to know that weekend in Atlanta. The self-assured young man doing what he loved—flying planes—and the vulnerable little boy whose devotion to his brother tugged at my heartstrings.

How could I not love them both?

Breckenridge, Colorado

IT'S TIME TO PUT down the journal for the night. Indulging in memories, I'm surprised to realize it's past my bedtime. Clouds are gathering, and when I close the deck door off the bedroom, I smell hints of winter in the crisp air. Almost without thinking, I pull one of Sam's faded chamois shirts from the closet, cloaking myself in the softness of the fabric, his familiar scent bringing him close. Sam. I can't wrap my mind around his unfaithfulness or his out-of-hand rejection of his son. But, despite everything, I miss him.

In bed, Orville nestles beside me, purring contentedly, and my thoughts drift as I feel my eyes close. A shrill ringing drags me back to full consciousness. Groggy, I glance at the clock: 1:10 a.m. I grab the phone. "Hello?"

"It's me, Iz."

"Sam, are you all right?"

"I knew I'd wake you. But—" and here I sense his internal struggle "—I needed to hear your voice."

Irritation and relief war within me. He could've stayed home and listened to anything I might have said. Or maybe that was the problem—he would've heard more than he was ready to handle.

"Sam, I don't know what to say. Unless you're ready to talk about all of this."

"I can't."

So here we are again. Sam stonewalling, not willing to share his emotions. I clutch the phone and sink back against the pillow. No words come to me.

"I shouldn't have called. It's late."

"It's okay." Then in a halfhearted attempt to lighten the mood, I say, "What's a wife for, anyway?"

Silence hums through the phone line.

I gather my courage. "Have you decided what you're going to do?"

He waits a beat. "It's not that easy."

I want to scream across the miles. Instead I swallow my hurt and disappointment.

"Izzy…I'm so sorry. I don't deserve you."

My baser nature tends to agree with him, but that's the part of me that fails to understand Sam is my world.

"The girls?"

I'm not up for casual conversation. "Both okay."

"And you? How are you really?"

I bite my lip in irritation. "How do you think?"

"I'm sorry," he says again.

In any marriage, there are the inevitable regrets, some more damaging than others. "I suppose you are," is the best I can offer.

I'm only now aware of how much has been left unsaid between us through the years. It had become a habit to skate over the surface of our relationship rather than tend to the brittle hairline cracks.

"I'll let you go now," he says wearily. "But I couldn't sleep without telling you one thing. No matter what, Izzy, I love you. I always have." His voice breaks. "I always will."

The phone goes dead before I can respond. Truthfully, I'm relieved. I wouldn't have known what to say, but Sam's final words remind me why I'm still here. Why I'm willing to wait for him.

Springbranch, Louisiana
1961

THE MORNING CAME FOR me to take the bus from Springbranch to join Sam in Tucson where he'd been assigned for advanced flight training. Mother fixed a big breakfast, slamming about the kitchen, banging pots and pans in thin-lipped disapproval. I was too young, then, to read hurt rather than anger in her jerky movements, too self-absorbed to put myself in her place and understand her worry. I don't recall what, if anything, we said to one another, only that our communication was hopelessly strained.

I do, however, remember what my father said. Before he drove me to the bus station, he invited me into his study. Taking his customary place behind the desk, he gestured me to the armchair at his side. Before speaking, he removed his spectacles, cleaned the lenses with a crisply ironed white handkerchief and settled them back on his nose. "We don't know your Sam," he began. "Or his people. And that is upsetting to your mother."

I waited, mute with the dread of disappointing him.

"But that's not so important for me, because I *do* know you. You are kind and would not willingly inflict hurt. I have strived to teach you the importance of being true to yourself." He looked intently at me. "Does this young man complete you?"

I managed a teary smile. "Yes, Daddy."

"Love." He said the word as if it were an enigma. "I believe it's the most important thing in life."

An overwhelming sadness crept over me. Had he ever known love in his own life?

In an apparent non sequitur, he continued. "How baffled Mr. Barrett must've been by the romance between his invalid daughter Elizabeth and the poet Robert Browning." My father smiled wistfully. "But see how that turned out."

He reached in a desk drawer and pulled out a small leather-bound volume. "May this gift be a constant reminder of the beauty and power of love."

I took the book into my hands, caressing the

soft brown leather as I read the title. *Sonnets from the Portuguese.* Elizabeth Barrett Browning.

"'How do I love thee? Let me count the ways,'" my father began.

I joined him, a solemn promise passing between us. "'I love thee to the depth and breadth and height my soul can reach…and, if God choose, I shall but love thee better after death.'"

My father nodded in satisfaction. "I'm proud of you, Isabel, and wish you much happiness."

My wonderful, quiet, unassuming father, unlike my mother, could let me go.

Davis-Monthan Air Force Base, Tucson, Arizona
Fall 1961

NAIVE? IDEALISTIC? BESOTTED? I was all of that the day I stepped off the bus and into the arms of my handsome, young husband and buried myself in his suntanned arms. Ever after, I've always found home in Sam's sheltering embrace. That morning Sam had only enough time before reporting back to base to settle me in our one-bedroom, unair-conditioned apartment. And to make love to me in a brief, ecstatic reunion. Afterward, rolling onto his back, he pulled me close and whispered, "Until I met you, I never believed in happy endings, never thought I deserved one. But, God, I do now." Those words bound him to me in a new and wonderful way.

Showering quickly, Sam put on his uniform, and with a lingering kiss, left me alone in the apartment in a place where I knew no one. Still flushed from our lovemaking, I explored my surroundings. The bathroom, tiled in mustard-gas green, was tiny. The west-facing kitchen boasted a small refrigerator, an ancient oven and a two-burner electric cooktop. The living room furnishings consisted of a vinyl couch, a two-person dinette set and one scuffed armchair. Sam had, however, added two large fans and a small black-and-white TV.

I peered into the refrigerator, wondering if I was expected to cook dinner. Then I unpacked, and was overcome with shyness when I discovered drawers filled with Sam's undershirts and briefs, a razor and shaving cream on a bathroom shelf and a pair of dirty jeans in the clothes hamper. Somehow I was to make this drab box a home for both of us, preparing appetizing meals, laundering military uniforms, keeping house. I lay across the utilitarian tan bedspread, immobilized by the enormity of my new role.

Until I heard a knock. I smelled the cigarette before I opened the door. There, one eyebrow cocked in assessment, stood the woman who was to become my chain-smoking, dyed-blond guardian angel.

Flicking her ash, she sized me up. "Honey, you look like you're straight off the banana boat." She moved past me into the living room and only then stuck out her hand. "I'm your next-door-neighbor, Marge DeVere. And I'll lay odds, you need help." She took a drag from her cigarette. "Am I right, sugar cakes?"

All I could do was nod. Marge was as unlike my sorority sisters or the matrons of Springbranch, Louisiana, as anyone could imagine, but I couldn't have been more pleased to see her. "I'm Izzy," I said, surprising myself. I had always referred to myself as Isabel. "And to tell you the truth, I don't have a clue." I shrugged, then grinned. "About anything."

Marge's laugh rolled up from her belly and filled the room. I joined in until tears ran down my face. Finally, catching my breath, I remembered my manners. "Please sit down. I have more questions than you can imagine."

"I've got plenty of time. Why don't you check the fridge and let's have us a beer and some girl talk."

Until then I had never guessed beer could substitute for an afternoon glass of tea. I pulled out two bottles, snatched up a bag of chips and settled on the sofa. In a few short hours she gave me a tutorial on the intricacies of being a military wife, reminding me to wear a hat and gloves when Sam and I called on his commanding officer and his wife, and cautioning me about speeding on base, an infraction for which Sam could be reprimanded. Never, before or since, have I been so grateful to a teacher.

CHAPTER FOUR

Breckenridge, Colorado

THE FOLLOWING MORNING when the phone rings, I am ill-prepared for my daughter Lisa's outburst. "Where's Daddy? I've tried his cell, his Blackberry... It's not every day his grandson scores two goals for his little league soccer team, and you'd think he'd want to know. But he's incommunicado, just when I need him and..."

I listen, wondering why the urgency. Scooter, Lisa's only child, is seven. Sam will be pleased and proud, but Lisa will not be satisfied because his reaction isn't immediate.

Our younger daughter is high maintenance, especially since her divorce. She harbors expectations—especially of Sam—but no matter what we do, we fall short. As a child, she kept us off guard, craving attention on the one hand and shrugging it off on the other. She adores her father, but it's always been hard for her to trust his love and approval. After leaving her husband a year ago and relocating to Boulder, she turns to Sam for all her honey-do's. Even though we understand her stress and vulnerability, sometimes we dread her phone calls.

She finally stops talking. I struggle not to make excuses for Sam's absence, which is, at the moment, none of her business. "Daddy's at his buddy Mike's Montana cabin. Fishing."

"When will he be back? Scooter keeps asking about him. Besides, something's the matter with my dishwasher."

I smile in recognition of her modus operandi. Scooter's alleged disappointment is the guilt trip; the dishwasher is the primary concern. "I'll have him call when he gets home."

We chat about Scooter's parent-teacher conference, and I suspect I'm hearing the edited version, the one that omits his mood swings. Lisa and Scooter have not had an easy time since her ex-husband remarried in an embarrassingly short time after their divorce. Thankfully he left Lisa financially secure.

"Dare I hope you have a full-blown case of cabin fever?"

"Not really," I murmur, surprised by the truth of my answer.

"Well, are you free to come stay with Scooter?

My baby-sitter has flaked out, and I have to be in Pueblo tomorrow."

I love my grandson, but find myself resenting the abrupt end of my solitude and the way Lisa takes me for granted. "I'll drive down this afternoon and we can have a nice dinner together."

"Only if you cook it. I haven't had time to go the store and won't today, either."

Lisa has an uncanny way of orchestrating life to accommodate her needs. Yet in truth, being a single mother is no picnic. She works a demanding job at the University of Colorado and as far as I know, scarcely has a social life.

"Remember, Scooter doesn't like cheese."

Scratch the macaroni and cheese. "How does he feel about meat loaf?"

"Haven't a clue. We'll see, won't we?"

We complete the arrangements, I fix a quick sandwich and pack my bag, pondering whether I should let Sam know that I'm going to Lisa's. I decide against it. If he wants his privacy, I'll give it to him. Besides, I really don't want to talk to him.

When I load Orville's dish with cat chow, he eyes me accusingly, sensing I'm abandoning him. "Back soon, kitty," I say, grabbing my keys and heading out the door. On the drive, I drink in the beauty of the mountains, now dressed in fiery aspens, resplendent against the dark blue-green of the fir and spruce. I'm reminded that we are living Sam's dream. Growing up on the barren plains of eastern Colorado, he loved the distant, snowcapped peaks, a shining El Dorado. In summer, dust swirled around the trailer house where he lived, and in winter, wind-driven snow formed impassable drifts. Early in our marriage he confided that his goal was eventually to live in the Rockies. His expression the day we moved into our Breckenridge home with its larger-than-life view of the mountains said it all. This is where I belong!

Stopping at the market, I pick up ingredients for dinner, and by the time Lisa and Scooter arrive home, a meat loaf and baked potatoes are in the oven and green beans are simmering on the stove. Scooter gives me a hug, then settles in front of the TV while Lisa changes into jeans and a Colorado Buffaloes sweatshirt. Then she pours us a glass of wine and sits on the sofa, legs crossed. Even though she looks tired, she is still strikingly attractive. "I know life isn't easy for you just now," I begin, "but you're a beautiful young woman with a full life ahead of you."

She stares at me, incredulous. "Just stop it, Mother, okay? I know what you're thinking—that I'm going to meet someone. But what man wants to take on another man's son?" With a toss of her head, she adds, "Besides, I'm too busy with my career and Scooter for a relationship."

It's as if she's steeled herself against further rejection. To see her pain and hear her interpret my advice as interference leaves me feeling helpless. I search for a safer subject. We talk about her work and Scooter's soccer until dinnertime—when all hell breaks loose. "Mamaw, what's this stuff?" Scooter asks, probing the meat loaf. He takes a tentative bite, screws up his face and says, "This is yucky." He looks at his mother. "Do I hafta eat it?"

"Scooter, mind your manners. Your grandmother made that especially for you."

He folds his arms across his chest. "I don't like it."

"It's one of Papaw's favorites," I offer as inducement.

"Don't care." His lower lip protrudes and tears gather on his thick lashes.

Lisa rolls her eyes. "Please, Scooter. Apologize to Mamaw."

He throws down his napkin and runs from the room, slamming his bedroom door behind him.

Lisa's shoulders slump and, for a moment, she looks desperate. Gathering herself, she says quietly, "Mom, sometimes I just don't know what to do with him."

"This is about more than meat loaf, isn't it?"

"I'm afraid so. He still doesn't understand why his daddy's gone. He blames me." Now her eyes cloud over. "It's so unfair. I'm not the one who walked out on this marriage to be with someone else."

All I can offer is a platitude. "It all just takes time, honey."

We eat our supper in silence. After dinner I leave Lisa to clean up the kitchen, and go to Scooter's room. "May I come in?"

He is sitting back against his pillows, holding the bedraggled Denver Broncos teddy bear he's had since infancy. I settle beside him, gathering him close.

"I'm sorry, Mamaw." I can barely hear him.

"I know. I thought you'd enjoy the meat loaf."

"I never had it before." He sniffles. "It's just that everything's different."

I rub my hand over his soft hair. "Life's like that sometimes. Things change and it takes a while to get used to the idea."

"Don't like change."

"It makes you sad, doesn't it?"

"Yeah." A long minute passes. "But I'm getting better." He snuggles closer. "Someday I promise I'll eat your meat loaf, Mamaw."

THE NEXT MORNING WHEN I return to Breckenridge, I call Twink at her New York City apartment. I need to hear a friendly, adult voice. I launch into an Erma Bombeckian recital of my time in Boulder. Twink's merry laughter raises my spirits. "Izzy, you are a born storyteller. It can't have been that bad."

"Says who?"

Then Twink does what she is so good at—asking the big question. "You're really concerned, aren't you?"

"I don't know how to help Lisa. She's a beautiful young woman, but she's let that ex-husband do a number on her."

"This isn't about you, and it's not up to you to fix it. She's an adult."

"I know, but I still worry."

"Look, she has to find her own way, just as I did when you tried to discourage me from marrying husband number two. Good old Stan. Nobody could tell me I was making a mistake. Not even you. Give Lisa some time."

Changing the subject, Twink tells me about the new Broadway season and a recent Greenwich Village art exhibit. Her life, as always, is light-years removed from mine. Twice divorced, Twink is worldly and cosmopolitan, while, despite all our travels with the air force, I still regard myself as a small-town girl.

I tread delicately into the next subject. "How is

your mother?" Lost in the fog of Alzheimer's and unable to recognize her daughter, Honey Montgomery lives in an assisted-living facility near Twink.

"The same. Mother was always glitz and style. To see her now, her mind gone, living as a captive in a body that refuses to die…it's nearly intolerable."

"Oh, Twink, I wish I were closer."

"So do I." Her voice trails off. "So do I."

I deliberate whether to tell her about Sam and me, but now is not the time. Not for her, and not yet for me.

"Enough of the pity party," she says. "Tell me how the memoirs are coming. Are you including the juicy parts?"

I manage a laugh. "I hope you're prepared for an exposé of our coming of age in Springbranch."

"You wouldn't!" I sense her grin over the miles.

"Don't bet on it. Remember the time when…" I launch into one of our more questionable escapades. By the time we hang up, I'm once again grateful for such a friend.

Davis-Monthan Air Force Base, Tucson, Arizona 1961

WITH MARGE DEVERE'S HELP, I purchased curtains, pillows and throw rugs that, along with the few wedding presents I'd had shipped to

Tucson, slowly made the apartment ours. Back then, I didn't know it was unusual for a man to notice each decorative addition, but Sam did and was pathetically appreciative. I found out why one night as we lay snuggled in bed following an especially satisfying lovemaking session.

"Thank you," he whispered.

At first I thought he was referring to the wonder of mutual orgasm, but then he went on. "I now have a real home, Izzy."

Turning toward him, I studied his face, sculpted by moonlight and shadow. "*We* have a real home," I corrected.

"You don't understand. You always had a home. I never did. Until now." He stared out the window, as if gathering his thoughts. "Home is a place you can't wait to get to. Where you know you'll be safe. After Mom died, that trailer we lived in reeked of cigarettes, booze and rancid food. The only decorations were empty liquor bottles and tattered *Playboy* magazines. If anybody swept up the trash and did the dishes, it was me. I dreaded going home. Why do you think I played every team sport there was?"

I buried my head in Sam's shoulder so he wouldn't see my tears. Our cramped apartment was basic, borderline shabby, temporary, yet for him it was a palace. "Do you feel safe here?"

He gathered me into his arms. "You're the

reason I feel at home." Then he chuckled. "Even with those pink floral towels you fancy."

"No self-respecting Southern lady could decorate without her l'il ole flowers."

His hand strayed down my arm and found the curve of my hip. "I love you, Izzy," he whispered, hugging me closer.

"And I, you."

From that night on, wherever we were stationed, I tried to make a home for my husband, a man who'd spent of his childhood without one.

MILITARY LIFE WAS CULTURE shock, and without Sam and Marge, I might have fled. Men were everywhere. Now, that might sound obvious, but my father had never been a guy-guy with a cadre of golf buddies, so nothing had prepared me for the sheer testosterone-driven energy of an air force base. I wasn't ready for backyard barbecues with kegs of beer and hearty male laughter, command appearances at the officers' club where young lieutenants stood three deep at the bar, or off-duty poker games featuring braggadocio and cigars.

With time, I came to understand how the camaraderie with its in-jokes, creative nicknames and backslapping was a hedge against the serious task in which the men were engaged. Against the fear that lay too near the bone.

Once I asked Sam if flying ever frightened him. "The flying itself is exhilarating. I love it," he said, "even though the responsibility for other lives is sobering. But fear? That's not a word I let myself consider."

Or speak to me about. Only once in our early married days do I remember him letting down his guard.

He'd come in from a training run, stripped to his shorts, crawled into bed and thrown his arm over his face. When I asked if he was sick, he waved me off. "Give me a few minutes."

Sam's customary exuberant homecomings always made me feel like a princess. Never before had he marched past me, shut me out like this. I sat quietly in the living room ignorant of what was wrong or what, if anything, I should do. Finally as the sun disappeared and twilight sent long shadows across the floor, I slipped into the bedroom and crawled in beside him.

"I'm not asleep," he said after a few minutes.

I snuggled in the crook of his arm and lay my cheek against his chest. The drumbeat of his heart did nothing to allay my concern. Somehow I sensed I should not speak. Outside the apartment, I could hear mothers calling their children in from play. A jet screamed overhead. The only evidence that Sam was aware of my presence was his finger tracing circles on my arm. We stayed like that for a long time. Suddenly the words erupted from deep in his gut. "Hotrod bought it today."

At first I thought I had misunderstood. John "Hotrod" Newcomb was one of Sam's closest buddies. Young men weren't supposed to die on training missions. To speak my dread in that moment was beyond me.

"Nose-dived into the desert."

"Oh, Sam." I sat up and for the first time looked into his eyes. The expression I saw there made an old man of him. "Can you tell me what happend?"

He began hesitantly, as if uttering the words would make the end result permanent in a way just thinking about it couldn't. They had been flying in formation when Hotrod experienced a mechanical malfunction. The plane went into a roll, then spiraled out of control. "It happened so fast," he said. "One minute he was flying off my left wing and the next the aircraft plowed into the ground, engulfed in flames. There wasn't anything Hotrod could've done." He beat his free hand against the mattress. "Goddamn it! It's not supposed to happen like that!"

"I'm so sorry. So very sorry."

He pulled me closer and, like a man possessed,

made love to me as if he might never have another chance. For all my innocence, I understood. He'd had his first brush with death at the hands of a military machine. Burying himself in me was a way to prove he was alive.

Later I suggested he invite some of the other pilots over for dinner the next night. I'd prepare the meal and then slip out to a movie. Many months afterward he told me how much he'd appreciated my sensitivity in knowing the guys would need to unload about Hotrod and even begin to laugh again as they recounted his antics.

After that night in bed with a brokenhearted Sam, I never forgot that what he loved doing was also dangerous and that, despite their bravado, none of those young pilots was invincible.

My concern for all of them and for our country escalated in October of 1962 during the Cuban Missile Crisis. Air force planes flew twenty-four-seven during those tense days when the United States faced the real possibility of nuclear war. Tension and fear were palpable among the worried families. All any of us could do was huddle by our television sets and pray.

Not for one minute after that did I forget that Sam was a warrior.

McDill Air Force Base, Tampa, Florida
1963

IN WHAT BECAME A WAY of life for us, no sooner did I feel settled in Tucson than we were transferred to Florida. By then, though, Marge DeVere had taught me that all of us wives were in the same boat and the only choice was to begin again at each new posting. She was right about one other thing: as the years passed, I came to regard my air force friends as family.

I was in need of such support that spring when I realized I was pregnant. We had waited for Sam to get this more permanent assignment before trying to start a family, but the immediacy of our success was a surprise. I'd expected to have months of leafing through baby magazines and reading Dr. Spock before being faced with an actual baby. The relationship with my own mother was still strained, but even had it not been, I wouldn't have turned to her with my questions. Sam's commanding officer's wife was another of my air force guardian angels. She treated me like a daughter and shepherded me through the entire pregnancy—from morning sickness to delivery— and set an example I later tried to emulate with Sam's junior officers' wives.

There were no early pregnancy tests then, so I

waited to tell Sam until I was absolutely sure. Our duplex had a small patio out back, bordered by palm trees. One evening as the sky faded from rose to purple to deep blue, we sat in our canvas lawn chairs, the silence between us comforting and restful. For all of Sam's exuberance and activity, I had come to recognize his need for quiet. Picking up my hand, he tilted his head back and contemplated the stars emerging one by one from the darkness.

At times like this we never needed words. I always felt included in his reverie. Rubbing a hand over my still flat stomach, I imagined the tiny being taking shape within me. Boy? Girl? With Sam's ocean-blue eyes? Or my brown ones? For a few moments I longed to keep the changes in my body secret, to revel in the wonder—just baby and me.

Sam pointed to the sky. "A shooting star." He straightened. "And another." Turning to me, he went on. "I love flying at night. Sometimes it feels as if I could reach out and touch the Milky Way. Pretty darn amazing." Kissing my fingers, he started to stand.

I tugged on his arm. "Don't go in."

Looking quizzical, he sank back into his chair.

"Just a little longer," I said, breathing deeply to dissolve the bubble of excitement rising in my throat. Softly, I began. "I know something else that's pretty darn amazing. A miracle, in fact."

He chuckled. "Oh, so it's miracles now, is it? Even better than the night sky?"

"Infinitely."

Something in my voice must've tipped him off, because he reached again for my hand and gazed deep into my eyes, a smile teasing his lips. "Izzy?"

My eyes filled, and all I could do was shake my head up and down. "Yes," I finally managed to say. "You're going to be a father."

Sam leaped from his chair, pulled me up into his arms and held me tight against his chest. "My God," he whispered. "A baby!" He repeated the word, as if to convince himself.

"Are you happy?" That question must be a universal reaction of the newly pregnant, but I so needed his assurance that having a child at this particular time was the right thing.

"Happy? That doesn't begin to get it." Then he held me at arm's length. "But are you all right? I mean, how do you feel?"

"I'm fine. A little morning sickness, but the doctor says I'm as normal as apple pie."

"What do you want? A boy or a girl?"

"A healthy baby. What about you?"

He raked a hand across his buzz cut. "Wow, I don't know. I'd probably be better with a boy.

Doing the sports thing." Inexplicably, his expression sobered.

"What is it?" I asked.

"I haven't had any experience being a father. And I sure as hell didn't have a good role model."

His bitterness and vulnerability broke my heart. I took his face between my hands. "Sam, you are not your father."

"But what if—"

"Stop it. You can be as good a father as you want to be."

"This is scarier than a full-scale dogfight."

"But a good kind of scary, don't you think? I've dreamed of carrying your baby. We can do this."

He cradled me to him again, his fingers playing through my hair. "My Izzy," he murmured against my ear, and though I couldn't be sure, I thought I felt his tears dampen my cheek.

ALTHOUGH I HAD NEVER met Sam's brother Lloyd, we had talked many times by phone. In late summer he graduated with a degree in English from the University of Colorado and took a teaching position at a high school in Billings, Montana. Sam and I had scrimped to supplement his undergraduate scholarships and to fund his plane ticket to visit us for Thanksgiving.

The Thursday before Thanksgiving I was sitting

at the kitchen table poring over cookbooks, in anticipation of preparing my first traditional holiday meal. I vacillated between cornbread or wild rice dressing, pecan or pumpkin pie. Intent on menu-planning, I was mildly annoyed when the phone rang. It was Twink. When I began the conversation, she barked at me. "Turn on your TV. President Kennedy's been shot."

I leaned back into the kitchen counter, cradling my abdomen, dizzy with incomprehension. "When? How?"

Then she told me about Dallas, the parade, the open car. Through the medium of the telephone, we clung to each other in disbelief. Awful things have happened to our country since then, but in those days the assassination of a president was unthinkable.

The joyous reunion with Lloyd took on a somber, reflective tone as the three of us watched Walter Cronkite chronicle this most shocking week, yet being together during that time made us an immediate family. Although Sam and Lloyd shared idealism and a commitment to service, they were very different. Bookish and witty, Lloyd charmed me with his references to literature and history. After Sam reported for duty the last morning of Lloyd's visit, he shared things about my husband I had not known.

"Sam was always the athletic one, the most-likely-to-succeed type. I have no idea how he kept up his top grades, because when he wasn't at practice, he was cooking, fending off our father's violent alcoholic fits, doing laundry, whatever. He probably hasn't told you that he was always the one who went to my school conferences and took me every Saturday to the library. If it hadn't been for Sam and my books, I don't know what might have happened to me. I owe him everything."

The story made me love Sam all the more, even as it filled me with sadness for the boy forced to become a parent. Sam rarely spoke of his childhood, and when his father died from liver complications in a VA hospital during the first year of our marriage, Sam's reaction had been relief rather than grief.

During those stark days following November 22nd, I learned an important lesson. In the big scheme of life, pecan pie or pumpkin—it doesn't matter.

BY EARLY DECEMBER, well into the ninth month of my pregnancy, I was waddling like a stuffed goose and counting the days until the birth, apprehensive as I was about going through the experience. Sam suggested I call my mother to come help, but I couldn't bring myself to do it. Less than enthusiastic about the baby, she still acted as if my marrying Sam was a personal affront. I resented her for not giving my husband a chance.

Instead I called Twink. We had not seen each other since my trip to Atlanta. Too long. She had recently married Bryce Gates, a wealthy South Carolina investment broker in his forties who traveled extensively. "I'd love to come," she said.

"Will your husband mind?"

"He's gone all the time. Why should he care?"

Her cavalier tone should've alerted me to problems, but I was too consumed with my impending motherhood. "If you're sure it's all right, I'd love to have you here."

"There's just one thing." Twink paused, then giggled, a sound I remembered so well. "'Miss Scarlett, I don't know nothin' 'bout birthin' no babies.'"

I couldn't help chuckling. "We'll learn together, then." Recalling our long-ago educational discovery in the Montgomerys' gazebo, I added, "Maybe we'll find another instruction manual."

I worried about whether Sam would be available when I went into labor. Military wives were supposed to understand that air force missions took priority over births. Jenny, however, had the good sense to arrive on one of Sam's weekends off. He stayed by my side, his expression tortured as I moaned and howled. This man who was always in command, who had stood up to his father and raised his brother, was unable to do anything but grip my hand. "Izzy, I'd do it for you if I could," he said, wiping my forehead with a cool cloth. As delivery neared, he was banished to the waiting room, as was the custom in those days, where, his buddies later told me, he paced like a wild man.

A true confession. Although Sam hadn't said anything, I had assumed he'd want a boy. During my pregnancy, I had called the baby Buddy, so sure was I that I would produce the son and heir. It seems ridiculous now, but I was shocked when the doctor held up Jenny, and said, "You have a beautiful baby girl."

"A girl?" I gasped. "That can't be."

The doctor chuckled. "Maybe you'd better take a peek."

Far from being disappointed, Sam gathered our darling Jenny in his arms, tucked the pink blanket around her light head of hair and tried manfully to choke down his sobs. Finally he was able to speak. "She's a miracle. Thank you, Izzy." In a move as unexpected as it was tender, he handed our daughter to me, then pulled the billiken from his jacket pocket and placed it on his daughter's tummy. By his ear-splitting grin, the figurine assured me that things were as they ought to be. I believed him.

"Sam, what a lovely gesture."

He winked. "Thought you might like it." When he leaned over to kiss me, those gorgeous eyes were deep wells of love. "God," he murmured, stroking Jenny's cheek with his forefinger, "I need to learn to take care of her."

And he did. Dirty diapers, formula preparation and all. My favorite memory of Jenny's infancy is Sam lying on the sofa with the baby on his chest, the two of them nose to nose studying each other intently. She was his new love, but he didn't forget his first one. The diamond engagement ring he hadn't had time to buy when we were married was my gift. Inscribed in the band were the words "Ever my North Star."

CHAPTER FIVE

Breckenridge, Colorado

I PUT DOWN MY PEN AND gaze idly out the window. Recording Jenny's birth should have been a joyous recollection; instead it raises questions. How did Sam's affair start? Was Mark's mother a North Star, too? What if he'd known Mark's mother was pregnant? Pain slices through me, made all the more acute by the happy memories of our early married life when it would never have occurred to me to question Sam's love or faithfulness.

How dare Sam run off to Montana without talking about all of this? Just walk away and leave me with nothing but wild suppositions? Damn it, I'm furious with the man. Yet at the same time I miss him. My Sam.

Desperate for some fresh air, I fetch my coat and set out on a walk, heedless of the brisk mountain temperature, the scent of pine or the dark clouds massing over the mountains. I walk faster and faster, as if by sheer energy I can hasten Sam's return so we can get to the bottom of this madness. Rounding the last curve on the way home, I suddenly remember that Jenny is coming for another visit tomorrow. She called yesterday with the excuse that she wants one more glimpse of the aspen, but I know she's checking on me. I'll put on a happy face and reassure her, but for once, I'd prefer she not come.

What I'd prefer is to continue losing myself in the happier memories I'm writing about. Even knowing that they won't last.

McDill Air Force Base, Tampa, Florida
December 1963

TWINK'S VISIT WAS A godsend. Between us we managed to keep Jenny bathed, fed and cuddled. That is, when we could wrest her away from Sam, who doted on her. Sam and Twink dealt with the cooking and laundry so I could regain my strength. Though tired, I moved through the days in a cocoon of bliss.

One joy of that period was watching Sam and Twink. Her devil-may-care attitude delighted him. She could hold her own with any man and gave him as good as he dished out. I remember vividly their debate one evening over the merits of their recipes for margaritas. They decided to test them both. You can guess who gave Jenny her bottle that night.

The afternoon before Twink left for home, she sat rocking Jenny. "I can't bear to leave her," she said in an unusual display of emotion.

"You could have your own," I suggested.

For a moment she stopped rocking, then, as if catching herself, started in again. "I don't think so," she murmured, turning her face toward Jenny.

"Why ever not?" My mind raced. She'd said all the right things about her wedding, Bryce, the life she led in Columbia.

"Could we please change the subject?"

"Twink, for heaven's sake, what is it? You can tell me anything."

She looked up, her face drawn. "And ruin our visit?"

"You couldn't ruin our visit. But something's the matter, isn't it?"

Then the barricades came down. "You have no idea how I envy you." I waited, and she went on. "You're so normal. Sam adores you. He loves this baby. He'd do anything for you."

My throat hurt. Softly I asked, "Is it Bryce?"

"God, what I mess I've made." She blinked tears away. "It all seemed so perfect. The society wedding, complete with a chamber orchestra and champagne for five hundred. A town house and a plantation home in the country. A bloodline dating back to Jefferson Davis." She snorted. "What was I thinking?"

It was my turn to ask the question she'd asked me months ago. "Do you love him?"

"I thought I did." She hung her head. "He's a marvelous dancer, an entertaining conversationalist. We had fun."

"But…"

"He can't have children."

My jaw dropped. "Twink, my God. When did you find out?"

She rubbed her hand over Jenny's back. "I thought something was wrong with me. I was ready to be tested when he told me about his practically nonexistent sperm count."

"He knew?" I was outraged.

"All along."

"Isn't that grounds for divorce?"

"And have the world know I'm the most gullible woman ever to come down the pike? No." She shook her head vigorously. "I'll stick it out. But that's not the worst. He has women on the side."

No gazebo education on a hot summer day had readied me for such revelations. My heart ached for Twink, but I had no idea what to say.

"It's okay, Isabel. I'm making the best of it for

now. Eventually, I'll probably divorce Bryce." She lowered Jenny to her lap and studied the rosebud of a face. "You'll never know what it means that you invited me to come here. This little sweetie will just have to be my baby, too."

That's when I asked Twink to be Jenny's god-mother. And when I learned that all the money in the world couldn't buy the happiness Sam and I shared.

Breckenridge, Colorado

I HEAR JENNY ARRIVE shortly after breakfast. Dressed in formfitting jeans, fashion boots and a bright yellow sweater with her blond hair tied back in a ponytail, my daughter looks more like a teenager herself than the mother of two. She's brought some special coffee blend and puts the pot on immediately.

"How was your drive?"

"Breathtaking. The slopes of Pike's Peak were butterscotch-yellow."

I put out some blueberry muffins and over our first cup we catch up on her family. With concern in her eyes, she finally says, "Mom, how are you? It worries me that you're here by yourself."

I smile fondly. "Baby girl, I've been alone before. Remember the times your dad was away on temporary duty for weeks at a time?"

"I know, but you were young then."

"And how is that different? Think of all I know now."

"I've insulted you."

I take her hand. "I appreciate your concern, and you're right, I'm not getting any younger. But in truth, I'm rather enjoying the solitude. The journaling is keeping me busy."

"I'm so glad. Honestly, I didn't know whether you'd really do it. Thank you."

"Don't thank me yet." Because my need to tell the truth has won out over self-censorship, I'm not sure I can ever give this memoir to the girls.

"How far along are you?"

"You've just been born."

"Could we look at the old snapshots?"

We spend half an hour poring over her baby photos, an act that transports me to a place long ago and far removed.

Jenny turns the final page of the album and looks up. "How's Daddy's fishing trip going?"

Little white lies don't count, I decide. "He's having a great time. Catching lots of fish."

"When's he coming home?"

I can't tell her I don't know. "When the trout stop biting, I imagine."

She sets the album aside. "Have you talked with Lisa?"

"Not since I went to Boulder several days ago. Why?"

"I don't know if I'm supposed to tell you, but she's met a man. An older man."

I blink. "She hasn't said a word to me. How long has this been going on?"

"Not long. Maybe a couple of months. But I'm worried."

I groan inwardly. "Go on."

"He's fifty-three, divorced, with two grown children and three grandchildren. I gather he has quite a bit of money. He takes her fancy places."

"You aren't impressed?"

"Don't misunderstand, I want her to be happy. But…I don't know quite how to say this. It's like she's looking for a father figure."

I wish I were surprised. I know Sam loves Lisa, but he's been a different person ever since he returned from Vietnam. Detached and remote… and unable to bond fully with his second daughter. Lisa's been trying to connect with her father all her life. "So, is it serious?" I ask Jenny.

"I think maybe it could be. Except for Scooter."

"Scooter?"

"When he met this man, he threw one of his tantrums. I hope she's not jumping from the frying pan into the fire."

"Me, too. But what can I do about it? If she doesn't tell me, I'm not invited into the loop."

"I don't know. It's just that she's so vulnerable right now."

"At least she's opening up to you."

"Do you suppose Daddy would talk with her? He's the only one who might get through to her."

A lump forms in my stomach. "All I can do is pass on what you've told me. Any conversation is up to Lisa and him. But interference in her life has never worked in the past. Besides, are you so sure this relationship couldn't be a good thing?"

Jenny nods thoughtfully. "I've considered that. But, Mom, it's so soon and what with Scooter's reaction, well, all of it leaves me unsettled."

Feeling overwhelmed, I sigh. "In fairness, we need to withhold our judgment."

After Jenny leaves for home, I'm struck by how quiet the house is. The silence I have treasured now seems empty. I need Sam.

McDill Air Force Base, Tampa, Florida
Mid 1960's

MY MOTHER AND FATHER came to visit for Jenny's first birthday. I scrubbed every nook and cranny, making the house suitable for Mother's scrutiny. This was only the second time since our marriage that Sam had spent any time with my parents. Mother was civil, if not generous, to him, full of child-rearing tips for me and charmed by Jenny. Between my stress level and Mother's controlling ways, Sam and my father provided a calming influence. In fact, the two of them quite hit it off. They talked military history, toured the base and took Jenny to the park. My father's approval of Sam was a joy.

The highlight came at dinner the last night my parents were with us. Daddy stood to give a toast. "To my beloved daughter, to dear little Jenny and to Sam, the son I never had. Cheers." I couldn't look at my husband. I knew he needed a private moment to gather his emotions. He was somebody's son.

I'd like to say that Mother softened toward my marriage. She didn't; she tolerated it. It wasn't that she said anything, but the message came through loud and clear when she went on at great length about my Springbranch friends—their social successes, modern homes, upwardly mobile husbands and, above all, their contributions to the Springbranch Women's Club.

Our temporary housing and itinerant lifestyle came in a pale second. I hate to admit it, but I was relieved when they left for home. Not Daddy, though. Just Mother.

BUSY WITH A GROWING circle of young mothers with small children, base parties and Officers' Wives Club committees, at first I was unconcerned about news reports of a struggle in Southeast Asia to deliver a place called South Vietnam from the Communists. Because of Sam's work, I might have been slightly more tuned in than some, but I assumed it was a police action, involving only a few U.S. military personnel, until I heard about something called the Tonkin Gulf resolution, whereby the President was authorized to take all necessary measures to repel attacks on the United States. In March of 1965, President Lyndon Johnson ordered a bombing raid to be carried out by air force units already stationed in or near South Vietnam.

The mood on base changed. No longer was it a peacetime facility. Training missions took on graver importance and conversations in the officers' club were charged with purpose. Veteran air force wives betrayed their fears. Any day now our lives could change dramatically.

For some, they did. Painful partings became a fact of life as various aircraft squadrons were deployed overseas. Families packed up to return to their parents' homes. Sam was restless, like a finely tuned racehorse being loaded into the starting gate. I knew he wanted to participate; that was what he'd trained for. His time would come, but until then, each day took on special significance for me—it was one more day Sam was at home and safe.

In the fall of 1966, I missed a period. Then came the queasiness. I couldn't think about having another child with Sam possibly being called to serve in the escalating conflict halfway around the world. Even as I felt guilty for wishing I weren't pregnant at this particular time, it became apparent I was.

Sam guessed before I could tell him. "You look different," he said one morning when he came in from an all-night training flight. I was sitting at the kitchen table. He crossed the room, then tilted my head up. "Izzy, are you feeling okay?"

"Just a tummy bug." I pulled away and stood, busying myself wiping down the counter.

He followed me. "I don't think so," he said in a teasing manner. From behind, he pulled me against his chest and put his warm hands on my stomach. "You're pregnant."

I turned in his arms. "How…?"

He grinned. "You think I don't keep track of your periods?"

Making an effort to smile, I said, "Okay. I give up. You're too smart for me." Then my voice wavered. "Is it all right with you?"

"All right? All right?" He picked me up and

twirled me around. "I'm the luckiest guy in the world. A beautiful wife, a perfect daughter and now a son. I'm thrilled."

A son. Uneasy, I whispered in his ear, "You can't just order up a son, you know."

"Sure, I can. I need a little buddy to even the numbers with you girls."

"That's tempting fate." I couldn't put my finger on it, but there was a seriousness beneath his bantering that concerned me. "You do realize that I have nothing to do with determining sex."

"But I do." He patted my stomach. "He's in the oven."

"Sam, stop it. What's this all about? You said you didn't care whether Jenny was a boy or girl."

He shrugged, then turned away to pour himself a cup of coffee. The gurgling of the water heater, the ticking of the clock, the sound of Jenny singing to herself in her bedroom took on an ominous normalcy. I waited. Then I heard him say, "That was before Vietnam."

Instantly, I knew what he was thinking. It was more important this time for a child to carry on his name in case he…didn't come back. I couldn't stand it. I threw myself into his arms and buried my face in his chest. "My God, Sam," was all I could say. More than anything I wanted to give him that son, but I was helpless. This precious baby had already been created.

SAMUEL BLAKE LAMBERT, arriving a month early and weighing in at a mere five pounds, was born on D-Day, June 6, 1967. "My little fighter," Sam called him. My pregnancy had been uneventful, marred only by Sam's unwavering conviction that I was carrying a boy. I couldn't get him to lighten up about it, to the point I became paranoid about having a girl. Sam laughed and told me to trust in the power of positive thinking. Easy for him to say.

Whether it was because of Sam's need for a son or because Blake was such a tiny fellow, I was even more protective of him than I had been of Jenny.

Twink came again to help me. We joked about how we couldn't keep using babies as an excuse for getting together. Yet beneath the joking was that same somber mood I'd seen in her before. "Are things any better with the marriage?"

"I guess you could say so. I'm living proof that you can get used to almost anything." She shrugged. "We live in a kind of marital truce. He does his thing, and I do mine. We are pleasant to one another, we make the expected appearances at fund-raisers and weddings, and I spend his money freely."

"Oh, Twink, is that any way to live?"

"Think about it, Isabel. What would I do? Where would I go? My degree in art history isn't going to put bread on the table."

My patience snapped. Where was the independent, resilient Twink I knew? "Stop it right now. You are a bright, talented woman. If you divorced, you would get a handsome settlement. You can make a new life."

She ducked her head, then said, "I'm scared."

Those were the last words I'd ever expected to hear from her. "I didn't think there was much of anything that could frighten you."

She looked straight at me. "I've fooled you for a long time, then. You have no idea how I've envied you and your family. I pretended it didn't matter that my parents moved at the drop of a hat, won and lost fortunes and would rather put on a fabulous lawn party than celebrate my birthday." She paused. "I'm so tired of pretending."

I went to her and pulled her in my arms. "Shh," I murmured. "You've just lost your way. It's nothing we can't fix."

"It's the failure, Izzy. I can't face it."

Just then Jenny came into the room and threw herself at Twink. "I wuv you, Twinkie. Don't cry."

Twink pulled herself together, leaving our conversation unfinished. We had no opportunity to continue it before she left the next day. I hugged her and said, "Call me. We'll figure out something. No damn man is going to make my friend miserable."

She didn't answer except to whisper in my ear, "Isabel Lambert, I hope you know how lucky you are."

THEN MY LUCK RAN out.

But I'm getting ahead of the story. July 6th, the first month anniversary of Blake's birth, Sam came home with a Tonka dump truck. On August 6th, a fielder's glove, and in September, a football. He would sit with the baby in his lap telling him all about Roger Maris, Johnny Unitas and Bill Russell. I could've sworn that little guy understood every word. Once I asked Sam, "What's that all about?"

His grin was mischievous. "Guy talk."

Sam had been an attentive father when Jenny was born, but he was even more attached to Blake. One day we were sitting out in the backyard while Jenny splashed in her small plastic wading pool. Blake lay on his back on Sam's legs, waving his chubby little fists. "Atta boy. Already practicing that left jab."

I set down my glass of lemonade, enjoying a moment of absolute contentment, untouched by the specter of war. Jenny sprawled in the water, legs splayed. "Look at me, Daddy. I'm a mermaid."

"Good job." Sam sent her a thumbs-up.

"They're beautiful children," I murmured.

Sam rubbed a finger over Blake's cheek. "I told you so."

"Told me what?"

"That we'd have a son."

"And if we hadn't?"

"I would have loved a daughter, too." Then he gazed adoringly at Blake. "But this is special." He paused before adding, "I wonder if my father ever felt this way about Lloyd or me. I doubt it. Bastard."

"Shh, the children."

"Sorry. But I'll tell you one thing. Samuel Blake Lambert is always going to know how much his father loves him."

At such moments, I almost felt jealous of the bond Sam had already developed with his son.

"He'll make a great pilot."

"What makes you think he'll follow in your footsteps?"

"Maybe he won't, but, Izzy, I want the world for him. It hurts sometimes to love him so much."

All the tenderness Sam's father had denied his son poured forth into that tiny baby. Such devotion, so many hopes and dreams. Thinking about it now, I wonder if we were, indeed, tempting fate.

So here we are. I can no longer put off writing

about what happened even though I'm not even sure I can find the words. Heartbreak robs you of courage.

IT WAS A BEAUTIFUL LATE October morning with the bluest of skies, as if nature had given me a reprieve from worrying about Sam's upcoming orders, which, almost certainly, would send him to Southeast Asia. A soft breeze blew off the Gulf and sunlight dappled the dewy grass. Sam had left at dawn for the base, and I sat in the breakfast nook, nursing a cup of coffee and watching the neighborhood teenagers waiting for the school bus—the girls primping, the guys jockeying for position. I remember thinking how quickly time passes. Jenny was nearly four, and the days of her childhood were speeding by with astonishing rapidity. Although it would be many years until she was ready for high school, I imagined they would pass in a flash. It made me all the more determined to savor each day with my children and to be more conscientious about keeping their baby books current.

Usually either Jenny or Blake was awake by seven, but today they were sleeping late. I poured a second cup of coffee and took Jenny's favorite cereal from the cupboard. Blake, just beginning to eat pablum and pureed foods, was turning into a little butterball. He recognized all of us and grinned toothlessly whenever Sam entered the room. I loved this stage—the cuddly flannel pajamas, the sweet smell of powder, the little fingers twining in my hair, the melodic goos and coos. Had it not been for the looming threat of Vietnam, life would've been perfect.

Those were my thoughts that morning. From the children's bedroom, I heard Jenny climb out of her bed, independent even then. "It's morning, it's morning," I heard her croon. "Wake up, baby, wake up."

No matter how many times I had told her not to disturb Blake, she always did, as if the day couldn't officially begin until her playmate was awake. I took down a bowl and poured Jenny's cereal. She always came out of a deep sleep ravenous.

"Whatsa matter, baby?" I heard her say. "Wake up!" I set down the cereal box and started toward the bedroom. "Baby—" I heard her rattle Blake's crib "—it's morning. Play wif me."

Then, out of instinct, I was running. In the doorway I was momentarily dizzied by the kaleidoscopic images of stuffed bears, the colorful mobile hanging over the crib, the rocking horse in the corner. Jenny stood at eye level with her brother, tugging on his blanket. Gently, I pulled her aside and leaned over the crib.

The image confounds my memory even as I write, seared as it will always be in my brain and on my heart. There's no other way to say this. I rolled Blake over and I knew instantly. Our son was dead.

"MOMMY, WAKE BABY UP!" Only Jenny's voice kept me from collapsing to the floor. For the moment all that registered was the need to get my daughter out of the room, out of the house. I picked her up and ran outside in my pajamas and slippers, my brain refusing to function so set was it on the lifeless little body I'd left in the crib. I don't remember what I said to my neighbor, but one look at me must've communicated volumes. "Go, I'll keep Jenny as long as you need me to," I remember her saying.

Back in our house, I couldn't stop shaking as I picked up the phone and misdialed twice calling for an ambulance. Somehow, too, I managed to get a message to Sam's commanding officer. Then I must've made my way to the bedroom because that's where medical personnel and another neighbor found me, sitting in the rocker holding my son to my breast and keening his name over and over again.

I don't know how long I sat like that, but long enough for Sam to get home. He raced into the bedroom, took one look and slammed his fist into

the wall. "Goddamn it, goddamn it!" he howled.
One of the men led him from the room, while
another gently pried the baby from my arms.
When I tried to stand in protest, my legs wouldn't
support me and I sank back into the rocker,
suddenly nauseous. Someone—I don't know
who—helped me put my head between my knees
until the dizziness passed.

The next thing I remember is sitting in the
living room shivering, a blanket around my shoulders, listening to a chaplain from the base. Sam
stood ramrod-straight, his back to us, staring out
the window. Platitudes washed over me. "Nothing
you could have done." "He's God's little angel
now." "No one knows why these things happen."

I didn't believe any of what I was hearing.
There had to be an explanation. Something I
could've done. I'd been sitting idly sipping coffee
and enjoying the morning while my son was
dying. It was obscene. If I'd checked on the
children before fixing the coffee, if I'd gone into
the bedroom sooner, if I'd noticed a problem yesterday... The self-accusations thundered in my
brain, so it was no surprise when Sam finally
turned around and said, "Blake was fine when I
kissed him goodbye at four this morning. What
happened, Izzy?"

He never came right out and said he thought our

son's death was my fault, but his body language and tone left little room for doubt.

Now, forty years later, parents are more aware of sudden infant death syndrome. Even so, there remain varying opinions as to its causes. Parental neglect is not one of them. In those days, though, SIDS was a hideous, guilt-laden mystery. Regardless of what logic and medical advances tell me, I will always carry that shred of self-doubt.

Sam's way of dealing with the tragedy was to clam up and retreat to the base where he buried himself in work. Mine was to busy myself with mindless details, and, even then, I'd be in the middle of something and totally forget what I was doing and leave the project to wander aimlessly around the house. Neither of us was functioning in a healthy way. Grief support groups and family therapy weren't as widely accepted or available in those days. Like good soldiers, we were supposed to gut it through.

In those first hours and days, the one time Sam and I came together was when we had to tell Jenny. It was the only instance where I saw Sam tear up. "Blakie gone?" Jenny looked puzzled. "But he'll come home, right?" Friends, to whom I am still so grateful, kept her much of the time immediately following Blake's death, but I couldn't wait for her to return so I could cuddle her. And nights? I checked on her countless times.

In the dark of our bedroom, I tried to talk to Sam, but he turned away. The wall of his grief was impenetrable. After he finally fell asleep, I would move closer, gently spooning into his body. If he felt my need for him, he never let on. His distancing himself from me became a pattern.

The funeral was held at the base chapel. Lloyd made it, but even he couldn't get Sam to open up. Twink flew in for the service, as well, her face nearly as ravaged as mine. When the strains of "Brahm's Lullaby" issued from the organ, I turned to Sam, tears streaming down my face. He wrapped an arm around me and pulled me close, but even in that gesture I could feel the controlled rigidity of his body.

My parents came, and for once my mother's practicality and organizational abilities were not only welcome, but a godsend. It was she who packed up all the toys and baby clothes and redid the bedroom as Jenny's, she who fixed the meals and saw to the laundry, she who addressed the envelopes of the sympathy acknowledgment notes I was barely able to write. For once, she had no suggestions for me, as if she understood that mourning one's child has its own calculus.

My father's tenderness soothed us all. One treasured memory is of him sitting on the sofa with Jenny snuggled by his side sucking her thumb as he read poetry to her—A. A. Milne, Edward Lear, Shel Silverstein.

I'd like to say there's a magic formula to get one through something like this. There isn't. After a bit, my grief turned to anger, which I directed primarily at Sam. How could he shut me out? How was it possible for him to be so stoic? Why couldn't we talk? And always lurking at the edge of my consciousness was the unspoken question. Was it my fault?

The first evening after family and friends went home, Sam settled in his chair and flicked on the television. I bathed Jenny, read her a story and tucked her in. Reluctantly, I returned to the living room. The sight of Sam deliberately tuning me out was infuriating. I marched to the television, turned it off and stood in front of the set daring him to ask me to turn it back on.

"Izzy, for God's sake, I was watching—"

"I don't care what you were watching. And for God's sake, as you so delicately put it, and for Jenny's and mine, we need to talk about what's happened. In case you've forgotten, we're married. For better or for worse. No doubt about it, this is the absolute worst, but I'm sick of being treated like a pariah by my own husband."

Sam laced his fingers across his stomach and stared at me, his expression impassive.

Resentment tumbled out. "You're supposed to love me. I'm supposed to love you. Does that go up in smoke because we've had a tragedy?"

"I can't talk about this. Not now. Maybe not ever."

"Well, we jolly well can't pretend it didn't happen. And I'm sick of facing it all alone. Damn it, Sam, I need you."

His face contracted in pain. "Needing is too hard."

"Is that all you have to say?"

"Leave it, Izzy."

I whirled around and fled to our bedroom, gagging on salty sobs. I was so angry I seized the first object my hand settled on and flung it across the room.

The billiken bounced off the draperies, landing with a thunk on the carpet. The god of things as they ought to be. A distorted laugh ripped from my throat. How fittingly ironic!

I fell across the bed, aching to the depths of my womb. Life would never again be as it ought to be.

Just before Jenny's birthday, Sam was promoted to captain, at that point, a hollow victory. In December his new orders came. His F-4 Phantom fighter squadron was reassigned to Udorn Air Force Base, Thailand, the jumping-off point for dangerous missions over North Vietnam.

CHAPTER SIX

Livingston, Montana

SITTING ON THE DECK of Mike's cabin, nursing a Scotch and mesmerized by the cadence of the rushing river, Sam was surprised when a bedraggled dog came out of nowhere and plopped down beside him. Her red-gold hair was matted with dried mud, and she licked at a sore paw. "You look like you're a long way from home, girl."

The golden retriever mix sat up slowly, rested her chin on Sam's knee, then gave a shuddering sigh.

"I know the feeling, sweetie. It's a hard-knock life."

He wanted to shoo her away. He had enough problems. Yet there was comfort in hearing his own voice. Scratching the stubble on his face, he realized that so far he'd accomplished none of the soul-searching he'd set out to do, immobilized by a kind of psychic paralysis.

He'd escaped by shouldering his rod and reel

and spending his time fishing. Then later having a prolonged cocktail hour before firing up the grill, eating supper and turning in. With so much on his mind, he'd thought he wouldn't be able to sleep. Instead, it was like those times on R and R when he'd been dead to the world for hours on end. But he knew that when he awoke, he'd be haunted by Izzy's wounded eyes and the specter of his cowardice.

He slugged back his drink. *Tomorrow I'll think about the mess I've made. About...him.*

When he rose, the dog followed. "Hungry?" From the trash can, he pulled out yesterday's T-bone with meat still clinging to it. "That'll get you started." She carried it onto the deck and settled in a corner. Finding an old plastic bowl in the cupboard, he filled it with water and offered it to her. By the time he'd cooked and eaten the better part of another steak, the mutt was at his elbow, eyeing his dinner. Shrugging, he stopped short of finishing and gave her another bone. "This'll build up your strength for finding your folks." Which he devoutly hoped would happen.

However, the next morning, the stray was waiting at the door. Sam groaned. This meant a trip into town for dog food. But maybe someone had posted a Lost notice, and he could once again be by himself, responsible for no one.

He opened the door and knelt to rub the dog's head. When he chuckled sardonically at this turn of events, the dog raised her head and eyed him pityingly as if to say, "You're a poor excuse for a man."

"Yeah, you and everybody else." Hell, he'd let his entire family down. What kind of husband and father was he? "You've found a sorry port in the storm, girl."

In town, no signs indicated someone had lost a pet, and after a bath, the old girl cleaned up well. Sam decided to let her hang around until she went on her way again. Meanwhile, he found himself calling her Sally, a name surfacing from deep within. Sally was his mother's name.

Later, standing in the cold river, he cast his fly toward a deep pool and pictured his and Izzy's stone and cedar house perched on the side of a Breckenridge mountain, framed by welcoming spruce trees. The place he called home—with the woman who was his home.

Izzy. He drew a sharp breath against an overwhelming sense of failure. Did she know how much she meant to him? Could she possibly fathom that he'd friggin' lost his mind in Thailand?

He began to reel in. When this Mark Taylor appeared and Izzy learned about Sam's indiscretion, she should've screamed at him, pummeled

her fists against his chest, called him an unfaithful son of a bitch, anything except what she'd
actually done. Given him time.

Would she ever look at him again the way she
had on that long-ago night in Atlanta when he
could've drowned in her eyes? He shouldn't
have left home, but he couldn't stay. Not until
he faced himself.

THE NEXT MORNING, AFTER his pathetic late-
night phone call to Izzy, Sam spread her letters
on the pine table, arranging them in chronologi-
cal order. He doubted she knew he'd kept them.
But he had. And now, no matter how painful, he
was going to relive those distant days of the
late 1960s and confront the factors leading to
his infidelity.

The easy explanation was the stress of combat
and the availability of a woman as lonely and
hungry for the touch of a fellow human being as
he had been. But there was much more to it, including things he'd been reluctant to face—ever.

He picked up the first letter, postmarked Springbranch. He knew how difficult it had been for
Izzy to go home to her mother, who never quite
forgave her for marrying him. Little Jenny, with
her golden curls and huge brown eyes, had served
as the bridge between Izzy and Irene.

Darling Sam,

The hardest thing I ever did in my life was wave goodbye when you left Jenny and me here. A part of me died inside. Whatever strain there has been between us in these last few months, I do love you with all my heart.

You are doing what you believe must be done, and for that, I am proud of you. So very proud. The last thing I want is for you to worry about us. We'll be fine, even if living with Mother is its own kind of trial. Yet, as you know, it's important to me to make peace with her. What she did to help the two of us, well, afterward, makes being here easier. As you can imagine, Daddy is a mediating presence.

A bit about Jenny. She loves riding her tricycle up and down the driveway. Mother bought a plastic wading pool much like the one we had in Florida, so in the hot afternoons, all three of us sit in the water, Jenny laughing as she splashes us. The other evening before bed she put her hand on your photograph and said proudly, "My Daddy." No chance of her forgetting you. Nor will I, my love.

Be safe and feel our love surrounding you. Your Izzy

He folded the letter and slipped it back into its envelope, aware of how hard she'd tried with him. He wondered if a man can ever communicate to his loved ones the dichotomy of war: the agony of being away from family and the adrenaline rush of action.

He'd been gung-ho. All his training had led to that defining tour of duty. The pain of leave-taking was part of the package, as was the thrill—and fear—of engagement.

To drop into Udorn Air Base in those days was to enter a different world. Not only because of the Oriental influence with its exotic sounds, smells and tastes, but because the base itself was a self-contained unit dedicated to defeating the Vietcong. He'd slept to the accompaniment of planes taking off and landing, subconsciously alert for the inevitable order to scramble. Days and nights were interchangeable; the routine, mind-numbing.

He read several more of Izzy's letters. From the fourth slipped a faded Polaroid of Jenny standing on the front porch waving a flag. Izzy had written on the back, "One little American supporting the U.S.A."

He shut his eyes against the memory of newsreel footage of protest marches and the outrage he'd felt knowing his fellow citizens mocked the troops. How little they'd understood of the carnage of warfare and how their betrayal influenced morale.

Only in the ninth letter did Izzy make direct reference to Blake. Even now, Sam's mouth went dry, his brain in frantic retreat mode.

I found a little antique chest at the second-hand store on Main Street. It seemed the right container for Blake's baby shoes and favorite blanket and, oh, yes, the darling little baseball cap Col. and Mrs. Elton gave him. I laid his baptismal and birth certificates on top. We were so lucky to have him, weren't we? Even for so short a time.

Sam leaned back and expelled his held breath. It was so like Izzy to find the bright side, to rejoice in the few short months of Blake's life. He envied her. Never had he felt anything but mind-numbing rage, not at Izzy, but at a God who could so suddenly take his son. The death was fact, but he had never accepted it.

He stowed the letters he'd already read on the bottom of the stack in the lockbox. Others lay there, waiting. *Yes, damn it, I am a coward.* But even though he knew he would eventually have to deal with all the memories, he'd had enough for one sitting.

Sally pawed at the sliding-glass door, and Sam let her in. Coming to his side, she nuzzled his leg. Her silent affection touched him in ways too complicated to explore.

SAM AWAKENED BEFORE dawn to the sound of raindrops pelting against the window. He started a fire in the fireplace before making coffee. Sally had slept with him, so at least she was warm and dry. Soon the rain turned to sleet.

After breakfast he had no place to turn except to the memories he'd buried for years. To that awful day when Col. Elton relieved him of duty to race home to a horror beyond imagination. When he'd walked into that bedroom, something had snapped. What his eyes and ears took in never reached his brain; instead, with brutish instinct, he'd exploded in fury and denial.

From that hideous moment on, he'd closed down. Just at the time he and Izzy needed each other, he'd retreated. Lord, how she'd tried to reach him, but he couldn't let her in. Like an automaton, he'd gone through the motions of work, leaving early for the base and staying late. Coming home to that house, with its memories of Blake, was torture. Although he'd tried to respond to Jenny, he'd probably failed even in that. Duty to the air force and the release of flying were all that kept him sane.

How had Izzy tolerated him? Why hadn't she left? Pain and grief hadn't been his exclusively, and on some level he'd known that, but to let Izzy see him reduced to helplessness was unthinkable.

It was as if Blake's death had irrevocably shattered their happiness. Those few months before he'd left for Southeast Asia, they'd lived in polite coexistence, going through the motions, even making love on occasion, but without intimacy or passion.

In today's air force the brass would probably order him to a shrink, but nothing a professional could have said or done would have brought back his little boy. In ways that seemed perverse now, he'd been eager to go to war, to lose himself in routine and the sudden thrill of combat. In that alien environment were no reminders of an infant-size University of Nebraska T-shirt or a tiny hand grabbing onto his finger.

Izzy had kept trying, as her letters demonstrated. But the man who'd left for war and the man who came home to her were far different from the man she'd married.

So now…what should he tell her? How could they speak of it? What was to be done about a stranger whose very existence dredged up a shameful past? About a man who would never understand that Sam had only one son. And this stranger wasn't it.

When the sleet slacked off, Sally waited at the door, a pained expression on her face. "Okay, girl." He let her out and she was back momentarily. He, too, wanted to leave the cabin, to jog mindlessly down the road, each step taking him farther from the reason he was there. With a heavy sigh, he picked up the next letter.

ENDEARMENTS SURFACED throughout the day. "Beloved Sam." "My darling Sam." "Sweetheart." Had she really meant them, or had she pretended in the effort to keep their marriage afloat?

He racked his brain to remember what he'd written her, but all he could recall was self-imposed restraint. He couldn't open the wound of his grief. Instead he'd resorted to travelogues and witty accounts of the off-duty capers of pilots who substituted bravado for homesickness and drunkenness for fear. Izzy's letters were full of answers to his questions about Jenny—how tall she was, how quickly she'd learned her ABCs, how she'd kissed his picture every night when she said her "God blesses."

Izzy had said little of herself, perhaps to maintain the fiction that she was fine. Her life outside the house revolved around church and the Springbranch Women's Club's war efforts. But there were several milestones.

Twink is coming to visit! This will be her first trip back to Springbranch. I hope her idealized memories don't lead to disappointment. After the life she's led, this town will seem more backwater than ever. Jenny will love her "Twinkie's" attention. As will I. Although I've renewed some friendships here, no one is as close to me as Twink.

Thank God for Twink. She'd always been there for Izzy. He'd never doubted that Twink would continue to stand by her, no matter what happened when he returned home.

Sam, honey, Twink's visit was a lifesaver. I was finally able to laugh, really laugh again. Mother means well, but being with Twink was like floating high above the clouds. One night we bought a bottle of bourbon, sneaked past the house where she used to live and hid out in the backyard gazebo I've told you about. The moon was full and the scent of roses filled the air. (It would have been romantic if you'd been with me.) I paid for it the next day, but we drank and told stories until past midnight. Mother didn't say anything to us at breakfast, but I could tell from the way she ever so carefully set down our juice glasses that she disapproved of our nocturnal adventure.

That was one of the happier entries. Sam liked thinking of the two friends finding joy in reenacting the past. He and Lloyd had no such pleasant memories of their youth.

I don't want to add to your worries, but I think it's time I tell you about Daddy. He has been so tired lately and is having trouble breathing. He continues to teach at the college and insists on walking to work every day. Mother and I are very concerned about him. The doctor says it's his heart. He's been so good with Jenny and is such a comfort to me that I don't know what I'll do if something happens to him. Mother is being stoic, but I see the circles under her eyes in the mornings.

He stuck the letter back in the envelope and thrust it beneath the stack. Had he offered support? Sympathy? Or had her problems seemed far removed from the immediacy of the flight line? Living at home with her parents and grieving Blake couldn't have been easy for Izzy.

> I had a letter from Twink today. Her marriage is over. It was only a matter of time, but it's nevertheless difficult for her. Her husband isn't being cooperative, and she's worried about her settlement. In the long run, this is a good thing. She doesn't love him, nor he her. I hope someday she finds someone to love the way I love you, my darling. I miss you and pray you are safe.

At the time, he'd had trouble believing Izzy. How could she love such an insensitive bastard?

On the first anniversary of Blake's death, he'd anesthetized himself with Scotch, then the next day had flown a mission into the jaws of hell, not really caring if he returned.

The longer he was away, the more trouble he'd had remembering Izzy. Her photograph on his kit shelf was of little help; instead it was as if she were frozen at the time of posing. What was her laugh like? What did she take on her hamburgers? How had her warm body felt cuddled against his?

But he'd loved her. God, how he'd loved her. Without her, a yawning empty space had opened up inside of him that nothing could fill—not booze, the camaraderie of his buddies or even danger.

At a buddy's promotion party four months into his tour, he'd met Diane Berrigan, a nurse at the base clinic. She looked nothing like Izzy. Diane was tall, fair complected with silver-blond hair. The expression in her soft gray eyes was both gentle and world-weary. In that male-dominated, chaotic place, she projected serenity. In the midst of his personal storm, that calm had drawn him to her.

What was there to say? She made him forget.

Throwing his head back, he expelled a deep sigh. He'd blocked Diane from his memory for so long that bringing her back to consciousness was painful. Had he known he was doing wrong? Certainly, but the capacity for rationalization in a war zone is well-tuned. Most of all he'd needed oblivion, an escape bought with the guilt of adultery.

There. I've said it. Adultery. Diane hadn't been looking for anything permanent. Like him, she simply wanted to experience being alive in the moment in a place where, with a single explosion, you could be blown to eternity. She knew he was married with a child. "I'm not asking anything from you, Sam, except this." And she began undressing him, running her hands over places that tingled beneath her touch. Places he'd thought were dead.

They took precautions. She could ill afford to get pregnant and he wanted no entanglements. They rationalized careful sex with no strings attached was a safe outlet for their emotions. For once he'd started looking forward to something—times when they could hop a flight to Bangkok, find a hotel room and lose themselves for a few mindless hours. Although they tried to be discreet, their liaison had been no secret from those closest to them.

The immediacy of Diane had driven Izzy, Jenny and home further from his thoughts. Life before Udorn was like a stiffly acted technicolor movie of clean, well-dressed people blissfully unaware of problems.

The next letter stopped him.

Sam, oh how I need you tonight. I'm so lonely without you here in bed beside me. The days are getting longer and the nights seem interminable. Please be safe and remember how dear you are to Jenny and me.

Oh, God. Sally, sensing his distress, laid her head in his lap. How had he stifled these memories for so many years? When he'd finished serving his tour and returned to the States, he'd made a conscious decision to bury that part of his life, as if it had never happened. He owed it to his family to make them the center of his attention and not look back. Izzy was never to know he'd been unfaithful.

A bitter laugh escaped him. *Thanks a lot, Mark Taylor.*

THE RAIN STOPPED midafternoon and mist enshrouded the cabin, obscuring the riverbank. It wasn't yet five, but Sam poured himself a Scotch. What did this Mark Taylor have to do with him? For over forty years he'd been ignorant of his existence, so what could the man possibly need from him now? If Diane had wanted Sam to know she was pregnant, she could've told him. But maybe he should be grateful to her. His ignorance had preserved his family. Generous Izzy—she thinks I should meet Mark. To what end? A Hallmark father-son bonding experience? *When hell freezes.*

He tapped an ice cube, watching it bob in the amber liquid of his highball. He couldn't picture a family gathering where he would say to his daughters, "Guess who's coming to dinner?" He knew he was probably heartless, but what was to be gained by some awkward family encounter? With work, he and Izzy might survive this, but what about Jenny and Lisa? Their hero daddy with a secret son? Sounded like a tabloid headline.

Setting his drink down, Sam paced to the

window, watching a weak sun burn off the fog. As if his body could no longer contain his mounting tension, he threw on a jacket, whistled for Sally and left the house. But no matter how fast he walked, he couldn't escape his thoughts. There was no room in his life for another son. That title belonged to Blake alone.

Sam shrank from remembering the infant, but his gut screamed the name. He ran—faster and faster. A roaring sound thundered in his ears. His lungs heaved. The muscles in his legs tightened. Still he ran. Until, drenched in perspiration, he sank onto a fallen log, head between his knees, watching his tears fall to the wet, mossy ground and listening to the anguished rasping of his voice strangling on his baby's name.

The accusation came in the guise of his father's voice. *Sam, you're stupid, nothing but a failure. You hear me? You couldn't even save your own son.*

BACK AT THE CABIN Sam poured his highball down the drain, started a fire and settled on the sofa, forcing himself to tell the story to Sally, a listener who would be completely nonjudgmental. "It's like this. I didn't know I could love like that. In that little boy, I saw the promise of a childhood I'd only imagined and certainly never experienced. In him I saw Lloyd—bewildered, lonely, lost. And I saw myself—defiant, hurt, longing for a way out. With Blake, I could make everything right. He would be secure, happy and, most important, he would know he was wanted.

"Of course, I loved Jenny to distraction, but with her it was different. I coddled and adored her. A son I would mold into a confident young man who would be my companion, as well as my son. I could be for him the father I never had."

Sally cocked her head.

"Don't look at me like that. I know my dreams were idealistic and, in many ways, self-serving. But I wanted so much for that boy.

"That October day was surreal. From the base to our house, I must've driven sixty, but it seemed as if I was in slow motion. Finally I arrived. I tore down the hall, then stopped in the doorway of Blake's bedroom. The sight of my wife cradling our lifeless son drove me over the edge.

"I couldn't believe he was dead. And for what reason? No reason. You know how that feels? The truth is I went crazy. And you know what, girl? Maybe I've been a bit crazy ever since.

"Izzy doesn't get it. For me, the mere thought of calling Mark Taylor son, blasphemes Blake's memory."

The dog got up, stretched, then lay on the hooked rug in front of the hearth. Paws extended toward the fire, she stared at the flames, as if considering the story. Sam had thought it would help to say the words out loud. It hadn't. More than ever, he wanted to bottle up the painful memories.

For some reason, out of the blue, came the image of Izzy's blasted billiken. The rotund body, sly face and all-knowing eyes. How he must have laughed at them that autumn day and at their blind confidence in the gods.

CHAPTER SEVEN

Breckenridge, Colorado

BLAKE'S DEATH. SUCH a bleak chapter in our lives. Strangely, though, after I finished writing about it, I slept a full ten hours. Now, in the morning sun, the snowy mountaintops glisten like crystallized sugar. The kettle whistle interrupts my reverie and causes Orville to scuttle under the table. I pour boiling water over a tea bag and inhale the aroma that always transports me back to my mother's house. Tea was her comfort drink. A few hours after Grandmama's death I found Mother sitting in the living room, a cup of steaming tea beside her, a damp handkerchief wadded in her hands.

Carrying my cup into the family room, I decide I'm ready to write about that difficult year in Springbranch without Sam, when, in reality, I grew up. But the phone interrupts before I can start. It's Sam. Involuntarily my heart leaps.

"Good morning," he says quietly.

"Yes, it is," I reply. "Catching any fish?"

"It's been raining the last couple of days."

"Here, too." Ridiculous. We sound like people who are barely acquainted.

"Izzy, I'd like to come home."

As if I'd been keeping him away? "Oh? When?"

"Tomorrow. Early evening."

"I'll plan a dinner I can hold until you arrive."

"Thank you."

I wait for him to say something, anything about the issue looming between us. "I'll expect you then."

"One more thing. I'm bringing someone with me."

Bewilderment gives way to irritation. "Who might that be?"

"I think you'll like her." For the first time, his tone lightens and I imagine his smile. "Her name's Sally and she has a loving heart, four legs and a tail. She's a golden retriever stray who seems to have adopted me."

I sag against the counter. A dog? "Orville may get jealous."

"Sally will win him over in no time."

"Do we really need a dog?"

"No, but she needs us."

"I guess that settles it."

"I've done some thinking."

"And…"

"I know. I've shut you out of part of my life."

My gut reaction is to use one of Lisa's pet expressions, "No kidding, Sherlock." But I restrain myself. "Could you let me in now?"

He hesitates. "I'm going to try, Izzy. Be patient with me."

"Okay," I hear myself say even though I'm wondering whether I have any patience left.

"You're my rock, Iz. From the first time I saw you, I knew you always would be."

Filled with the emotions of a lifetime, I can't help myself. "I love you, Sam," I murmur before hanging up the phone.

I sip from my mug. Mother was right—tea is comforting, but not nearly so comforting as the news that Sam is coming home. Before he arrives, though, I need to write about Vietnam, an era that altered us and our relationship.

I am poised, pen in hand, when a random thought comes. Sally. He named the dog Sally. His mother's name. A piece of the puzzle that is Sam falls into place. He misses her still.

Springbranch, Louisiana
1967-68

GOING HOME TO SPRINGBRANCH was hard. My whole world collapsed with Blake's death and

Sam's aloofness. His orders to Udorn AFB, Thailand, nearly finished me. Before he left for Southeast Asia, we loaded up our Chevy and drove to Springbranch. I hadn't wanted to say goodbye there under my mother's watchful eye, but in an unusual display of tact, she gave us our space. Sam and I were tentative with one another. Still grieving Blake and terrified this could be our last time together, our lovemaking was both guarded and achingly poignant. And how very much was left unsaid.

Lloyd drove from Montana to pick Sam up to return to base. His worried look said it all. Time with Sam was precious, but at least the brothers had those hours together in the car. When Sam gathered Jenny in his arms for that final farewell, I could hardly hold myself together. Then he gazed over her shoulder at me, his eyes beseeching my understanding. In that glance, I knew that, despite what we'd been through since our son died, Sam loved me.

After he left, I quickly realized I had learned a great deal as an air force wife. I was far more independent, a trait honed by the times Sam had been away on missions. I could handle government forms, minor medical emergencies and the rudiments of car maintenance. Under my parents' roof, I was determined to be treated as an adult, especially by my mother.

Our first blow-up occurred the day she decided to cut Jenny's hair while I was at the supermarket. When I pulled into the driveway, a shorn Jenny came racing to greet me. "We played beauty shop. Look, I'm a pixie." She pirouetted, then clapped her hands. "Mamaw cutted my hair."

The curls? Where were the curls? I set down the sack of groceries and tore into the kitchen where my mother was peeling potatoes. "Who gave you permission to cut my little girl's hair?"

Mother turned around, a patronizing smile on her face. "I didn't know I needed permission. After all, dear, I cut yours when you were little."

"That's not the point." My face burned red. "She is my daughter. I will make those decisions." I glanced around, frantic with concern. "Where are they?"

"What?"

"The curls!" I snapped. "At the very least, I want to save a lock or two for her baby book. Maybe send one to Sam."

Mother's bland expression infuriated me. "You're getting upset over nothing. I threw them out."

I sucked air. "From now on, I ask you to remember I am Jenny's mother. Decisions regarding her welfare and appearance are mine. Please respect that."

"Well, I declare," she sniffed, before turning back to the potatoes.

I went out to the patio, picked up Jenny and ran my fingers through her soft, stubby hair. She felt strange, looked strange. From beneath a toddler's curls, a little girl had emerged.

Later in my bedroom, I stood in front of the mirror, studying my image, hunting for the backbone that had suddenly surfaced. Hardly ever, except for eloping, had I asserted myself with my mother. It was empowering.

Although the haircut confrontation was a small triumph, it set the pattern for our stay. Mother consulted me and even began to depend on me, particularly when Daddy's health deteriorated.

Evenings, I wrote Sam. I'd decided that my letters needed to be loving and supportive, despite the turmoil we'd recently been through. After Jenny was asleep, I would sit at the old rolltop desk in my bedroom and daydream about Sam. More often than not, it was the man I fell in love with who inhabited those dreams, rather than the husband of recent months. That was a blessing; it was far easier to write the old Sam. I could express myself in those letters in ways I hadn't been able to in recent months.

Mail from Sam came regularly and he said all the right things about missing Jenny and me, but there was a reserve I couldn't put my finger on. But then, what did I want him to do differently? Give detailed accounts of harrowing missions? Confess to fear? Describe hospital visits to maimed fellow pilots? Maybe the Sam I built up in my head was a fiction. I only knew I needed to cling to that image of him.

After weeks of accompanying mother to church and the Springbranch Women's Club meetings, I grew increasingly restless. It was Daddy who suggested I might take a course or two at the college, despite Mother's objections. Although my LSU degree was in English, I'd always thought about studying journalism. On impulse one day, I enrolled in two classes. Not only did the course work occupy my mind, but my fellow students provided a social outlet.

My class schedule permitted me to walk to campus in the mornings with my father. I treasured our stimulating discussions about politics, movies, books and current events. One morning stands out from the rest. We had just crossed the street headed for the humanities building when he stopped suddenly. His briefcase clattered to the sidewalk and he gripped his chest. "Call an ambulance," he gasped just before collapsing to the ground.

The rest of the day was a blur. A neighbor kept Jenny while Mother and I were at the hospital. A grim-faced doctor delivered the news. "He's suffered considerable damage to his heart. There's really not much we can do other than give him some medication and tell him to take it easy." Essentially, we took Daddy home to die.

It's not easy writing this, even now. My father aged before my eyes, his body gradually shrinking, loose skin hanging from his arms, his complexion ashen. Jenny was his sunshine. She would sit for hours chatting or watching *Captain Kangaroo* with him.

Oddly, Mother seemed to shrink, as well. She still kept Jenny while I was in class, but as soon as I returned home, she would go to my father. All those years I had convinced myself there was little love between them, but devotion is the only word to describe her care of him. One evening after I'd tucked Jenny in, I stole into their bedroom to say good-night. Fully clothed, Mother had fallen asleep in the bed beside Daddy, her hand clasping his. With a tender smile, he nodded at her. "She's a wonderful woman, Isabel." I blew him a kiss and left the room, infinitely wiser.

Increasingly, Mother abandoned her chores to me. I was grateful. There were few idle moments to indulge my grief for Blake or sicken with fear for Daddy and Sam. I was seeing another side of Mother altogether—her vulnerability.

My father's end came swiftly and peacefully. Blessedly, Jenny was at a neighbor's house. Mother sat on one side of the bed and I on the other. His labored breathing held us in thrall for several hours. And then…without warning, it stopped. Just like that. My mother, dry-eyed, efficiently covered him and left to phone the funeral home. She continued to function, even as if in a trance. I, on the other hand, flung myself across the bed, sobbing in paroxysms of grief.

We moved stiffly through the next couple of days. People came and went, their hushed voices and armloads of food constant reminders of our loss. Once again I had to explain to Jenny about death. Her tear-streaked face and tiny voice undid me. "Papaw's gone. He's wif Blakie, right?" She folded her little hands in her lap. "Far, far away. Where Daddy is."

To a child that connection made sense, I suppose. "No, honey, Daddy's coming back to us. Blake and Papaw are with God, forever and forever."

Her lower lip quivered. "That's too long, Mommy."

I cupped her sweet face in my hands. "I know, honey. I know."

When Sam got through a few days later, hearing his voice from halfway around the globe was such a comfort. "I know how much you loved your dad.

He was good to me. I admired him a great deal. But how are you doing, Izzy?"

The truth? The bottom had dropped out of my world, and I made it through each day only because of Jenny and by the grace of God. "I'm managing. And you?"

"It's hard. I wonder whether we're doing any good over here. The frustrating part is that there's no way really to tell."

"The protest marches can't help."

Bitterness edged his voice. "No, they don't."

We said our goodbyes and he talked briefly with Jenny. When she got off the phone, she smiled at me. "Daddy's not so far away. Not like Blakie and Papaw. I can talk to Daddy."

My body cried out with the need to talk to my daddy. Instead, three days later I took over the household when Mother fell apart. For several months, I planned the meals, did the laundry, cooked, paid the bills and gardened—all while going to school and tending to Jenny and my mother.

It's an unsettling feeling when you realize that in the blink of an eye, you have become your parent's parent.

Days fell into a routine, brightened by calls from Twink, journalism classes and the freelance work I did for the Springbranch *Courier*. Midway into Sam's tour, letters came less frequently and dealt with mundane topics like the personality of his new commanding officer or the menu for Thanksgiving dinner. Not one word about himself. Something was different. Was I over-reacting? Projecting the boredom of my own routine? I rationalized that his perfunctory tone and hollow-sounding declarations of affection were figments of my imagination.

I know now that they weren't.

Honolulu, HI
1968

TOWARD THE END OF Sam's service in Thailand, we met in Hawaii for his R and R leave. I imagined a romantic delayed honeymoon. Much as I wanted us to be together, I stewed over what to wear, what expectations he would have, how we had changed, whether we could bridge the gaps of time and distance. A bundle of nerves, I landed in Honolulu, clutching my straw purse, tugging at my mini-skirt and searching the lobby for his familiar face. Then I saw him striding toward me, his body leaner, his movements more controlled. He placed a fragrant lei around my neck, gave me a quick hug and a peck on the lips, then reached for my overnight bag. "You're going to love Hawaii,

Izzy." Then, with an arm around my waist, he ushered me toward the baggage claim area.

In the cab on the way to the hotel, I marveled at the palms swaying in the humid ocean breeze and the brilliant, multihued bougainvillea. "It's even more beautiful than I had pictured," I said.

"Let's make the most of our time here." Sam pulled a brochure from his shirt pocket. "There's a luau at the hotel tomorrow night, then I thought we'd take in the Pearl Harbor Memorial the next day. Maybe hop a plane over to Maui or the Big Island later in the week."

I remember staring at him in amazement. I didn't want a tour director, I wanted a husband. In a moment of daring, I had even gone out and purchased some sexy lingerie. When we arrived at our hotel on Waikiki Beach, I unpacked, then joined Sam on the balcony overlooking a serene Pacific. He stared at the horizon, hands thrust in his pockets. Tan and fit, he held himself stiffly. I stood beside him, unable to appreciate the beauty before me, so aware was I of the gulf between us.

When he turned, I noticed the lines etched around his eyes, the set of his jaw. Tentatively, I reached out and stroked his cheek. "I've missed you."

He picked up my hand, kissed it, then turned back to the view. "It's hard to believe you're really here."

"It does seem unreal." Despite all my self-talk about letting our time together unfold gradually, my stomach quivered at the detachment I detected in his tone. "Where do we start, Sam?"

"Tell me about Jenny," he said, turning and sinking into a lounge chair.

Had he deliberately misunderstood? I had meant how we could find our way back to each other. I pulled out snapshots of Jenny and told him about his daughter, embellishing to fill the time. In this manner the first awkward day passed. Although we made love that night, I had the distinct sense Sam was somewhere else.

I convinced myself that his abrupt transition from battle zone to tropical paradise explained his reserve. Oh, we had a good enough time—sightseeing, sipping mai tais, sunning on the beach. But our laughter was hollow and forced; our conversations, stilted. He had changed, but was carrying on as if everything was normal. There was no mention of the missions over North Vietnam, of Blake…of anything that mattered.

By our last night I was so tense I could hardly think. I didn't want to confront him, not when I was sending him back into a nightmare, but I could no longer rein in my emotions. I wanted my husband, not this automaton. I slipped into the black lace baby-dolls I had saved for this moment. Sam sat on the balcony in his skivvies. My heart in my throat, I curled up in his lap and draped my arms around his neck. The bare skin of his chest sent delicious tremors through me.

"Izzy," he whispered, his voice thick.

"I love it when you call me that. Remember what you said that first night in Atlanta about Izzy and Sam, Sam and Izzy?"

"That seems a long time ago."

"Not so very long," I murmured, laying little kisses up and down his neck. "I loved you then and I love you now." I could tell he was aroused, but he said nothing, did nothing. I hesitated. "I guess I'm not very good at this seduction business."

Suddenly he pulled away, holding me at arm's length, studying my face. I felt exposed, embarrassed, tearful. "It's not you, Iz. It's me." Then he gathered me in a bear hug. "Please, it's not you. Never you." Comforted by the beating of his heart, I listened. "I can't explain. I don't know if I'll ever be able to." His voice dropped off. "A lot has happened…"

I understood that he had experienced horrible things that scarred a man for life. "You don't have to explain."

His voice caught. "I can't. Not now. Maybe never."

"I just want you home safe and sound."

He sighed. "I know. But if something happens…"

"Shh. Not tonight."

"No matter what, I need you, Izzy. I always will."

Then he carried me to the bed, luminous under

a full moon. I would like to say we made love. But we didn't. Sam was a man possessed, as if he would never again have sex. As if he needed to leave a mark on me, not just from the kisses with which he covered every inch of my body, but from the very force and power of his penetration. With each thrust he was saying, "I am here. I am here. Don't forget me." Finally he collapsed on me, sweat making our skin slick, the overhead fan stirring an erotic breeze. We fell asleep in each other's arms.

Sometime in the night, I felt Sam enter me again, his animal-like grunts seemed like cries of desperation. It was over quickly, yet I felt his imprint deep within me.

The difference between intimacy and sex was never more obvious than that night. I was female; Sam was male. It was as simple, and as complicated, as that. Only later did I remember he had never said, "I love you."

Nine months later Lisa was born.

Davis-Monthan Air Force Base, Tucson, Arizona
Post-Vietnam years

AFTER SAM RETURNED TO the States, we were assigned again to Davis-Monthan where Sam was an instructor. The routine of air force life was comfortingly familiar and helped overcome the natural estrangement between us. Other wives were experiencing that same awkward period of reconnection with their husbands. We knew it would take time, but I'd never anticipated how much.

I was four months pregnant when Sam came home. He doted on Jenny, but acted indifferent to the new baby inside me. In truth, I understood. Having lost Blake, I was petrified with fear. What-ifs abounded. Those same thoughts must've occurred to Sam, but we never voiced them, as if doing so would jinx our unborn child.

I tried to allay my concerns, but all I knew was that one minute Blake had been fine and the next he was dead. I clung to an entirely irrational thought: if this new baby was born healthy, then I would be forgiven for Blake's death.

All Sam ever said to acknowledge my pregnancy was, "I hope it's a girl."

For this delivery, the air force did intervene. Sam was on a flight when I barely made it to the hospital. An easy birth. Sam's wish fulfilled. Lisa Irene Lambert, eight pounds, eleven ounces.

Lisa turned out to be a fussy baby who mixed up her days and nights. Impatient with her crying, Sam wanted no part of walking the floor with her or giving her a bottle. "I'm better with toddlers," he explained. *Bull,* I thought to myself. From the time Jenny was born, he'd spent hours caring for her. When Lisa began walking and talking, his excuse was, "I'll keep Jenny out of your hair."

One day when Lisa was about eighteen months old, I lost it when Sam refused to change her diaper. "What is it with you? You give all your attention to Jenny. This little girl needs a daddy, too."

"Don't you think I know that? I'm doing the best I can." His voice took on a brittle tone. "I can only take so much, Izzy. Just leave it, please."

It was then I knew. Lisa represented something unpleasant for him—fear? guilt? resentment?—and he couldn't deal with it.

Mother was thrilled with her namesake. The new grandchild helped pull her out of mourning and restored her to her old self. As years passed, she routinely visited us for six weeks a year, even during our assignment in England. I took the girls home as often as I could. I wanted them to know Springbranch, still amazingly untouched by what passed for progress in larger communities.

Although Sam was never quite the same after the Vietnam War, I soon realized there was no point dwelling on my memory of the cocky, playful, sensitive man I'd married. I would catch glimpses of all of those traits in the older Sam, but I could see in him an even more pronounced melancholy. Over time, we readjusted. We made a commitment to go out one night a week, just the two of us. It was over these candlelight dinners, that I again saw love reflected in my husband's eyes. There was so much I admired about Sam—his air of command, his well-developed sense of right and wrong, his loyalty to his brother, his interest in the welfare of his men. But I missed the passion of our early married days.

As time went on he bent over backward to treat both girls the same, but Lisa's mercurial nature irritated him, as did her occasional tantrums. Yet no one could say he was not a good father.

I could go on and on about our post-Vietnam years. But it came down to this. With effort, we made a happy life together, buoyed by a growing network of air force friends. When I look back over the years, I can't imagine living without him. It's pretty amazing to think that one brief moment in Atlanta determined my destiny.

Periodically through the years, I've picked up the billiken, stared into that smug, elfin face and pondered the implications of "things as they ought to be." Does that mean we have the power to manipulate our lives to an end of our own choosing? Or that events beyond our control shape us? Do the gods know better than we what "ought to be"? Provocative questions.

Although both Sam and I put the Thailand year

behind us and overcame the strain it put on our marriage, I had never fully understood what happened to Sam over there.

Until Mark Taylor knocked on our door.

Breckenridge, Colorado

SO…I CAN NO LONGER avoid writing about Mark. It's nearly midnight and a cold north wind is howling around the house. Tomorrow evening Sam returns from Montana and the unraveling will begin. I don't know what Sam's decision will be concerning his son. But I am clear about mine.

Since the knock on the door that changed everything, I've run the gamut of emotions. Anger. Humiliation. Hurt. Resentment. Incredulity. I've wanted to throw things and to curl up in a ball. But then comes the ache of love and the need to forgive.

I recall Mark's troubled blue eyes, so like his father's. His understanding of my position. And his intense longing to connect with Sam. Mark didn't stay long that day, just long enough for me to empathize with his situation.

"Mrs. Lambert, I can't explain it, but from the time I was a boy, I always suspected Rolf Taylor was not my biological father. Make no mistake, I loved him and consider him my dad. He was very good to me. But somewhere out there, I knew there was someone else, someone more like me.

"Last year when Mom was dying of cancer, she kept calling me 'Sam.' At first I thought it was the delirium, but then I noticed that Rolf would leave the room when she did it. It became important to me to learn who Sam was. Please, I can't turn back now that I'm so close."

Mark had begun his search by confronting his stepfather, who acknowledged he was not the biological parent and had never known the last name of Mark's father. Finally, Mark succeeded in tracking down an old air force nurse friend of his mother's. She provided the "Lambert."

So that's it—Sam had an affair, and now we are all victims, Mark included. It's too late to pretend things are different. Lives are involved, and actions have consequences. Sam has a responsibility to this young man.

And so do I. Mark Taylor is every bit as much Sam's flesh and blood as are Jenny and Lisa. As was…Blake.

Help me, Sam. Help me to make sense of what happened… and what must happen.

Somewhere in the midst of all of this pain, I have to believe there's love. If only we can find it.

CHAPTER EIGHT

Livingston, Montana

AFTER LOADING THE SUV, Sam spread an old blanket in the backseat for Sally, filled a couple of water jugs and settled her for the trip home. He was dreading being cooped up with his thoughts for the long drive.

Once on the road, he phoned his brother, who, within minutes, recognized that something was wrong. "You sound weird. What's up?"

"Nothing much. I just needed a few days to myself." He paused. "I've been at Mike's cabin. Doing some thinking."

"Sounds heavy."

"Yeah, it is. Lloyd, what do you remember about our mother?"

"Jeez, I was just a little kid."

"I know. Can you recall anything?"

"She had pretty blue eyes and used to sing to us. Then she got sick, and I was always afraid I'd make too much noise or do something to make her worse. Or upset Dad."

"I was afraid, too. Every day. Like I'd swallowed a lead weight."

"I remember how you'd hide in the storage shed."

Sam straightened, puzzled. "What're you talking about?"

"You don't remember? Dad brooded and snapped at us, blaming us for everything that went wrong. I only felt safe when you were around. When I couldn't find you, I'd come to the storage shed. There you'd be—huddled in the corner, wrapped in an old horse blanket. I'd crawl under it with you, and we'd hum over and over again that lullaby Mama always sang when she tucked us in bed."

As Lloyd talked, Sam's memory kicked in. The dark shed, smelling of motor oil and grass clippings, the scratchy fabric of the blanket, the soothing sounds of boyish voices intoning, "Hush, Little Baby, Don't Say a Word." How could he have forgotten? Or more likely, blocked it out?

When he was silent, Lloyd filled the gap. "Hey, bro, why did you ask me about Mama?"

Sam snapped out of his grim reverie. "I've taken in a stray dog I'm calling Sally. That name popped up out of nowhere and, as a result, I've been thinking about Mama."

"It was a long time ago. It's not like you to revisit the old days."

"Damn right. I have few pleasant memories of those years."

"Tell me about it. But we came out all right, didn't we? You know, Sam, any good times from back then involve you. I could've turned out pretty badly, but you wouldn't let me. And you wouldn't let yourself. You set a darn good example."

Sam thought about the barren eastern Colorado landscape, the relentless heat and frigid cold and the small-mindedness of the townspeople. "We made it. By the skin of our teeth."

"And by the grace of God." Lloyd hesitated, then chuckled. "Hell, we're living proof of the American dream."

They turned the conversation then to the Denver Broncos' chances in the AFL West. Yet Sam couldn't help wondering if his subsequent actions hadn't made a nightmare of his personal American dream.

A COLD NORTH WIND buffeted the highway, and clouds massing in the west hinted of an early autumn snowstorm. Sam calculated the distance. With luck, he could get home to Izzy before any measurable precipitation. Izzy. She had every right to kick his butt from here to kingdom come.

He'd hurt her big-time, just as he had back in Honolulu when he'd been incapacitated by guilt. He couldn't have given her any answers then even if she'd asked. He'd been a clumsy, self-serving son of a bitch.

When he'd first seen her in the airport, his immediate instinct had been to run. She'd looked so beautiful, so trusting, gazing at him as if he were a hero. He couldn't take it. The only way to hold shame at bay was to keep busy, keep moving—when all he'd really wanted was to bare himself to her, not just about Diane, but about the fear that threatened to unman him each time he flew a mission over North Vietnam.

He'd known she wanted to talk about things that really mattered. Yet the kind of intimacy they'd had before Blake's death had died right along with the baby. Distance had only complicated the situation. During that leave, he and Izzy had circled each other, as if venturing too close to the truth would doom their fragile relationship. Throughout their time together, he'd had the uncomfortable sense of existing in two worlds and belonging in neither.

Then, that last night, when she'd come onto the balcony in that sexy black outfit, he'd about lost it. This was his wife, the love of his life. How could he have betrayed her? He'd loathed himself even as he'd wanted to bury himself in her and never let go. When Izzy left the next day, it was as if everything good and pure in his life had stepped on the plane with her.

When he'd returned to base, he'd written Diane a letter breaking off their relationship. He had never heard from her again.

With the passage of time he'd deluded himself that his indiscretion was buried in the past. Until a few days ago when a stranger appeared claiming he was Sam's son. A son he didn't want to meet, didn't want to deal with.

As if in sympathy, Sally stirred, stood on her hind legs and licked his neck. Pulling into a rest area, he let the dog out for a run. The first pricks of icy rain hit his face. His jaw tightened. He needed to get home to the only person who might somehow be able to accept him, flaws and all.

DRIVING THROUGH DENVER rush hour traffic, Sam noted the temperature hovered just above freezing. Rain glazed the streets, and it would soon be snowing. On the north side of Denver, he dialed Lisa's Boulder home, hoping conversation would ease his nerves. "Dad-dy! Could you circle by here on your way home? Scooter would love to see you, and I can use help with the dishwasher. It's on the fritz. Here's what happens when I try to turn it on—"

Ever since her divorce, Lisa had been particularly helpless about certain things. She probably hadn't considered the inconvenience of a Boulder detour.

"Not tonight, honey. I'm heading for the barn."

"But it's snowing in the mountains. You could spend the night here."

She didn't give up easily. "Your mother's expecting me. Besides, I have Sally with me."

"Who?" She spoke so loudly that the animal in question cocked her ears.

"I'm bringing home a stray I've adopted."

"A dog! Scooter will be thrilled."

"Is he there? Put him on."

She called the boy to the phone. "Papaw, I scored a goal yesterday." He gave an account of his soccer exploits. Then he said, "Mommy says you're coming to see us."

He gritted his teeth. Lisa had set the kid up. "No, son, not this time. I have to get home."

"But Mommy says—" His voice turned whiny.

"Put your mother back on."

"Dad, why did you upset Scooter?"

His fault, just like everything else. "Once and for all, I am going home tonight. You can hand-wash the dishes. I'll be down to help in a couple of days. Talk to you later." He hung up before she could start in again.

When Izzy had written him that she was

pregnant with Lisa, a result of their time together in Hawaii, he should've been ecstatic. Instead, he'd been seized with fear. And anger. He hadn't wanted another baby. There could be no baby but Blake. And he was gone. Sam had failed to protect him, and the responsibility of another life was more than he could handle. He'd prayed for a girl. That way, at least, there would be no damaging comparisons.

He'd known he disappointed Izzy. He'd been a lousy father to Lisa and had been paying for it ever since. From the time she was tiny, Lisa had gone out of her way to get his attention, resorting to screaming fits and acts of teenage rebellion. But loving her too much was scary. What if something happened to her as it had to Blake?

An unsettling realization swept over him. Lisa had been as much a victim of Blake's death as he was.

Nearing the Eisenhower Tunnel, the rain turned to sleet. Turning up the heater, he started talking to Sally primarily to avoid further introspection.

"It might be hairy getting home, girl, but I promise you'll like it when we get there. Izzy will love you, but it might take a day or two for Orville to warm up, but as cats go, he's pretty friendly."

When they came out of the tunnel, snowflakes as big as nickels danced in the headlights. The highway was a white ribbon stretching into the night. Up ahead Sam spotted the lights of a snowplow. After some slow going, Lake Dillon appeared on the left, and he knew he was nearly home.

Thick snow blanketed the roads, trees and houses as they approached home. Sam drove into the garage and closed the door behind him, but couldn't bring himself to move. A yip from Sally spurred him to action. Stepping out of the SUV, he slipped a leash over the dog's neck. Drawing a deep breath, he walked into the utility room. "Izzy, I'm back."

Dressed in faux-suede jeans and a turquoise cashmere tunic, his wife stood in the doorway, a stainless-steel ladle in one hand. The rich aroma of homemade vegetable soup filled the air. "I was worried," she said. "The weather forecast was ominous."

Neither of them made a move toward the other. In the awkward silence, Sally tugged at the leash and tried to skitter toward Izzy.

Izzy knelt, and Sam released the leash so the dog could go to her. "Sally, huh? A very fine name." Izzy set the ladle aside and ran her hands through the dog's coat. "You're a honey-love. Welcome to Breckenridge."

Just then a loud hiss caused all three to turn toward the kitchen. Back arched and ears flat,

Orville eyed Sally. At the same time that Sam said, "I'll take Sally out," Izzy scooped up the cat and departed for another part of the house. Sam frowned, hoping that Orville's and Sally's meeting wasn't a foreshadowing of his and Izzy's.

SAM CARRIED IN HIS BAGS, then the cooler. Izzy took off the lid and studied the trout. "These need to go into the freezer."

"I'll do it." He reached for the cooler, but she had already picked it up.

"Go unpack. Dinner will be ready in twenty minutes."

Like a kid banished to his room, Sam unpacked slowly, reluctant to finish before the appointed time because, sadly, he had no idea what to say to Izzy. Stepping to the window, he watched fresh snow blot out the landscape, wishing it were so easy to blot out the past. Orville hopped up on the bed, as if claiming his domain. Sam mustered some humor. "You been sleeping with my woman, buddy?"

Ignoring the question, Orville opened his mouth in a gigantic yawn, then lay prone in the middle of the bed Sam hoped he'd share with his wife tonight.

"Dinner, Sam." Izzy spoke from the doorway.

"Smells good." He trailed her to the breakfast

room table, set with colorful Fiestaware. Slowly they began to talk. First about Sally, then about Jenny's visit. Fish tales carried them through the homemade apple pie.

Sam helped clear the table, aware that it was an attempt to ingratiate himself with Izzy. By the way Izzy prolonged loading the dishwasher, he figured she felt as awkward as he did.

"An after-dinner drink?" he offered.

Folding the tea towel over the rack, she turned to him, her expression neutral. "Kahlúa and cream would be nice."

He fixed the drinks and joined her in front of the fireplace. Sally, feeling at home, settled at his feet. Logs crackled and sparks flew up the chimney. "They're predicting six to eight inches," Izzy said.

"Significant for the first of the season." Silence.

It didn't take a genius to see that she was waiting for him to take the initiative. The long drive, the warm soup and the Kahlúa wrapped him in a comfort he was loath to disturb. Nevertheless, he began. "I know we need to talk."

"Yes, we do. A great deal depends on where we go from here."

"Before we even get to Mark Taylor, we have to talk about Vietnam. Diane. What happened."

She nodded. "Our troubles began before that."

He knew she was alluding to Blake. "Please, not tonight."

"I understand. You're tired. What's one more day among so many years? Tomorrow?"

"Tomorrow." The promise eased the tension in his chest, even as he dreaded facing up to the past.

Izzy sipped from her drink. "It hasn't been all bad, Sam." In her eyes he found wistfulness.

"What?"

"Our marriage. Ever since Vietnam, you've been an attentive husband and father. We've had some truly good times."

"But what you're saying is that it can be better?"

"That's my prayer. Only time will tell."

"You know…tomorrow? Um, it isn't going to be easy."

"I don't expect it to be."

He took their empty glasses to the kitchen. When he returned, she'd tucked her feet up under her and was staring pensively at the fire. Orville, sitting on her lap, regarded Sally with disdain. "You'd better get some sleep," Izzy suggested. "I'm sure the drive was tiring."

She had left him with no clue about tonight. "Uh, where do you want me?"

She looked up, surprised by the question. "Why, where you belong, Sam. In our bed."

Relieved, he longed to reassure her that all

would be well. But he was in no position to make promises.

In bed, he tossed and turned for an hour until Izzy slipped between the covers. Just knowing she was beside him was soothing, and within minutes, he fell asleep.

THE NEXT MORNING SAM sat at the head of the breakfast room table with Izzy to his right, each fingering a mug of coffee. Outside a pristine layer of snow, untouched except for occasional animal tracks, spread to the tarn, where wisps of condensation obscured the water.

Izzy began. "Did you love her?"

He struggled with the truth. "Never like I've loved you."

"That's not a no then?"

"It's more complicated than that."

"Help me understand. I've never so much as entertained the thought of another man."

He spread his hands, palms down, on the table, willing the words. "Hear me out." He closed his eyes, conjuring up the nonstop activity that was Udorn, the claustrophobic cockpit of an F-4 Phantom jet, the dark tops of dense jungle foliage concealing all manner of danger and the gut-wrenching, endless days lived on the edge of sanity and panic.

"I've never told you the whole story of my time in Thailand. When I got home, I thought the manly thing was to spare you by keeping it to myself. Put simply, my air force brothers and I went through hell. That's as straightforward as I can be. I'm not saying this to win your sympathy or to excuse myself, but if you're going to understand what happened to me over there, this is an important part of it. You know how crazy I was about flying. As a kid, that two-bit airfield in eastern Colorado was my escape. I loved everything about the crop-dusters and single-prop puddle-jumpers that landed there. On my way to school each morning, I'd check the wind sock and imagine the day when I would file my own flight plan.

"When you met me, I was intoxicated with the freedom of flying and the satisfaction of realizing my dream. I'd left my old life behind and didn't have a care in the world. I didn't think things could get any better. Finding you was the icing on the cake. I felt invincible." He shook his head. "Flying missions over North Vietnam was something altogether different."

Finally he looked at Izzy, who sat very still, cupping her mug between her hands. He couldn't read her expression. "I'm listening," she said simply.

"Newspaper and television accounts didn't scratch the surface of what we went through. For some guys, booze and drugs were the only way to tolerate the horrors. Flying a plane was nothing compared to what those poor joes on the ground faced. Yet climbing into that cockpit took every ounce of nerve and willpower I had. All we could do to anesthetize ourselves from paralyzing fear was to maintain a cool facade and focus on the details—the maps, the instruments, the weather, the formations, the mission. Because hanging over us, suffocating us, was the continual threat of death. Your bowels turn to mush when you watch planes exploding all around you in the night sky or heading, nose-first, for the ground at hundreds of miles an hour.

"To befriend fellow pilots was to expand by a thousand-fold the agony of each loss. The only way to survive was with graveyard humor and half-assed boasting. No one said it out loud, but we were terrified, knowing each minute could be worse than the last. We were trained as weapons. The innocent thrill of a fifteen-year-old flying an old Piper Cub was lost in the sheer reality of piloting a killing machine."

"How many did you lose?"

Sam scrubbed his hands over his face as the ghosts of "Tank" Feldman, "Jolly Roger" Bateman, Boyd Helmers, "Batman" Robins and a host of others crowded his memory. "Too many to count."

"You stopped writing me about them after your friend Jake Addeberry was shot down."

"Yeah. You didn't need to know. You would just have worried all the more."

"I worried anyway." Her misty eyes fixed on him. "Every day I didn't see a chaplain walking up the front steps was a godsend." Then she cocked her head. "You're still living with it, after all these years."

The ache in his gut etched itself in his words. "You never forget."

"I suppose not."

He stared out the window, hoping Colorado's natural beauty would dispel the phantoms of his fallen comrades.

"Did you have close calls yourself?"

How much could he tell her? Was total honesty merely a means of self-vindication, or was it a part of his life she needed to know about? All he could do was nod.

As if sensing his reluctance, she placed a hand on his forearm. "Sam, this is a beginning. You've buried so much. Layer by layer, you have to let me in." She paused, obviously trying to gather her thoughts. "This is a marriage. Keeping our feelings to ourselves has preserved the illusion of intimacy. And maybe that's what we needed once. It's time now for the real thing."

"I love you, Izzy." The words, ripped from his heart, hung between them.

"I know." She removed her hand from his arm. "But sometimes love alone is not enough." She rose to refill his mug.

Sam put out his hand to stop her. "I want to tell you more, but I can't sit any longer. Are you up for a walk in the snow?"

"Yes. We could use some fresh air."

He tried not to read anything into that comment. In silence, they donned boots, parkas, gloves and headbands. When Sam let Sally out of the utility room, she bounded ahead down the driveway. Without conscious thought, as they had done many times before, Izzy walked on his right. Together, they stomped a track through the snow.

When they reached the road and headed for the tarn, Sam took Izzy's hand. Relieved that she didn't pull away, he inhaled sharply and began. "I had several close calls. Our missions were generally at night, and once we got over North Vietnam, surface-to-air missiles lit up the sky, sometimes missing us by mere inches, sometimes striking dead-on. The night before Thanksgiving, we lost three in our squadron. Heading back to base, we were caught in torrential rains. All I could see was the greenish-amber of the instrument panel and a cascade obliterating the windshield. We'd had to make several passes over the target, and my fuel gauge was registering dangerously low. I figured we had a one-in-ten chance of making it back to base safely. Then the nightmare started."

His palms were moist inside his gloves, and a slight vertigo that had nothing to do with the 10,000-foot elevation momentarily obscured his vision. Even now in Breckenridge, Colorado, his body tensed as he recalled the erratic hitch signaling engine trouble. Over the radio crackled the voice of his guy in back. "Hear it, Cap'n?"

"Roger that." Each mile from that point on was a race against engine failure and bail-out.

"Sam?" Izzy stopped, a concerned frown creasing her brow.

He realized then that he'd been transported to a world dozens of years ago and half a world away. "Sorry, I was just remembering."

Then, painful as it was, he told her about limping home in the crippled plane and landing blindly in a tropical downpour, the gas gauge registering empty. When he finished, Izzy said nothing. At the edge of the tarn, they paused. The sun had evaporated the mist, and the water was a mirrorlike blue. Izzy put her arm around him and rested her head on his shoulder.

"Why couldn't you tell me any of this when you returned from Thailand?"

A fair question. His chest ached with the truth. "I couldn't. Things were…different."

She pulled away. "That's what we need to talk about."

Whistling for Sally who was still romping ahead, Izzy hugged herself, then turned and started for the house.

Sam followed, each crunch of his foot in the snow reminding him that the war in Southeast Asia was over. The conflict in his marriage, however, was another matter.

CHAPTER NINE

Breckenridge, Colorado

SAM IS STILL OUTSIDE clearing the walkway and front porch. That's just as well. I need breathing space. How can he have walked around for nearly thirty years with so much bottled up inside? I wonder whether he'd ever have told me if Mark Taylor hadn't shown up.

In the kitchen, there's a blinking light and an unfamiliar number on the answering machine. Pressing Play, I turn to pour myself another cup of coffee. The voice filling the kitchen stops me. "This is Mark Taylor. You said you'd be in touch after you and your husband talked, but it's been a while, and I, um, wondered if I'd missed a message from you. Please call me."

Easing the phone back into its cradle, I stand quietly sipping coffee and gazing out the window, watching Sam shovel. I'm puzzled by the sympathy I feel for Mark Taylor, whom I barely know. Why should I be uncomfortable because he's waiting on tenterhooks? It's Sam with whom I need to concern myself.

When he finally comes into the house rubbing his hands and breathing hard, I'm sitting in front of the fireplace with my journal in my lap. Shrugging out of his coat, he points at the paisley-bound book. "What's that?"

"A journal. Jenny and Lisa have been bugging me to write my memoirs. While you were gone, I decided to make a start. Lots of memories to cover."

"Good ones, I hope."

"Many are. But if I gloss over the bad stuff, it won't be a truthful account."

He throws his parka across a chair and stands in front of the fire warming his hands. "Like Diane. And…Blake."

I'm surprised he brings up the two subjects he has so studiously avoided. "Yes."

With his back to me, I can't read his expression. "Vietnam was bad," he says quietly, "but Blake's death…" He stops, then clears his throat. "God, Izzy, I still can't talk about it."

His body is rigid, just as it was that long-ago day when we buried our son. I wait. Sally, entering from the kitchen, goes immediately to him and sits at his side, rubbing her head against his leg.

After long minutes the dog retreats under the

kitchen table. Finally, Sam turns around, his face flushed, and joins me on the sofa. "I can't bear to put you through any more pain, but if you're ready, I'll tell you about Diane."

I study the sparkling half-carat diamond on my ring finger. What wife is ever ready to hear about the other woman? His saying her name—*Diane*—is an obscene familiarity. But I have no choice. I must listen if Sam and I are ever to find our way back to one another. I wrap my arms around my waist, aware it is a futile attempt to clamp down the dread spreading like a cancer through my system. Unwilling to face him, I close my eyes, bracing for a story I don't want to hear, much less be part of.

"Look at me." He picks up my hand, dwarfed in his. "Please."

I blink away tears and lift my head. His expression is a study in remorse and sadness. He cups my face, and with a thumb, dries a wet place on my cheek. "Understand one thing, Isabel Irene Lambert. I loved you the first time I saw you, I love you now, and I've loved you every day in between." He kisses me on the forehead, then sits back, his fingers twined in his lap. "But, God I've made mistakes."

"Me, too," I murmur, thinking back to that young wife and mother who couldn't find a way through her own grief to help her husband with his.

"In fairness, Diane was more than a mistake. This is the part that will be difficult for you, Izzy. You asked me earlier if I loved her. I didn't answer you. I told you it was more complicated."

I watch Orville slink across the area rug, stop to size up the situation and then jump into my lap where he drapes himself across my thighs. I am grateful. He is something tangible to hang on to. "Go on."

"First let me say I never meant for it to happen. But in the middle of that hell, I was so damned lonely. I missed you and Jenny with an ache that never went away. And Blake? I couldn't even talk about him. God help me, when the guys would ask if I had kids, I'd say, 'Yeah, one little girl.' I never mentioned Blake. Sometimes flying through that inky sky, with missiles going off on all sides, I would wish for death, hoping to end the pain of losing my son. I went a little crazy over there. It was impossible to project even a day ahead. All I could do, all any of us could do, was live in the moment.

"Swear to God, home might as well have been Oz. It had no reality. Remember when we met in Honolulu? I could hardly adjust to the luxury, the cleanliness, the sheer indulgence of it. Caught up in the Vietnam madness, all of us guys needed somehow to prove we were alive wherever, however, we could."

I stroke Orville repeatedly, trying to put myself in Sam's position, trying to understand what would drive him to another woman. But even as my mind takes it in, my heart breaks. "How did you meet her?"

"At a promotion party at the Udorn Officers' Club. A buddy asked me and some guys from my squadron to tag along for all the free beer and drinks we could slug away and for a glimpse of the best-looking nurses in the Far East. The bachelors in our group were a helluva lot more interested in the women than I was. I staked a claim to a bar stool and watched the others dance and cut-up, getting drunk enough myself to find their antics diverting. Three seats down sat this soft-spoken blonde. She'd turned down her share of offers to dance when a bruising major, obviously pie-faced, pulled her from the stool and insisted she dance with him. She tried to get away, but he wouldn't let go. That's when I intervened. And that's how I met Diane Berrigan. She was a nurse at the base clinic and had seen heartbreaking and horrible things, just like the rest of us." An ember flared and crackled. The only other sound was that of Orville's purring. "Is this too much for you, Izzy? I can stop."

Of course, it's too much. And not enough. "Go on. I'd rather hear it all at once," I say, even as I know each new image will have the force of a body blow.

"She was quiet, kind of contemplative. And disillusioned. She had gone into nursing with big dreams of helping people, of watching them heal and be restored to life. But much of what she saw over there was one mutilated body after the next being helicoptered out. There was no opportunity to learn what happened to the young airman who lost both legs or the grizzled sergeant whose insides had been ripped to shreds. It was taking its toll on her. Even so, she had found what seemed like this reservoir of calm. I wanted some of that.

"It's important for you to understand. It wasn't sex or boredom that drew me to her. This may sound weird to you, but with her, I felt safe. Your letters were wonderful, and I knew you loved me. But you weren't there. She was."

I grip Orville so hard, he screeches and runs for the back of the house. "Damn it, Sam." I struggle not to cry. "Go on, get it over with."

He stands and crosses to the fire. With the poker he stirs up the ashes, rearranges a log, then merely waits, the implement still in his hand. "I don't want to hurt you like this."

I stand, too. "Don't you get it? It's too late. I hate this. I hate what happened. But more than any of that, I hate what we've become. This false life we've been leading. And ultimately there's the really big question, isn't there? What we do about your son."

"I told you, Izzy. I don't have a son."

"Oh, that's wonderful. There you go again. Into your famous denial mode. Sit down." Like a commanding officer, I point to the sofa, and he takes a seat. "Now hear this, Colonel. You are going to tell me all of it. Right now. And what's more, when we finish this chapter of your life, we're going to face the next one. What you do about Mark Taylor, who, whether you like it or not, is every inch a Lambert."

I am shaking, but my outburst feels satisfying. I'm not going to put up with evasions, half-truths and omissions in the interest of preserving Sam Lambert's ego. He will lay it all out or I'll march. I love the man, but I will no longer sacrifice my feelings on the altar of his.

"I didn't love her, Izzy. I loved how she made me feel."

I can't bring myself to sit next to him. Instead I ease into my favorite chair, that distance between us buffering me from the attraction I feel for him even now.

"It started simply enough that evening with a few drinks. When she wanted to leave the party before her friends did, I walked her back to her quarters. I liked it that she didn't feel the need to talk all the time. The silence was companionable. I told her all about you and Jenny. There was no misunderstanding about my married status or my devotion to you."

"Then…why? I don't get it."

"The best answer I can give you is that I needed a friend who didn't rely on me and who asked for nothing in return. She was someone I could go off with for a few hours or days and almost forget where I was. We both understood there was no future."

"You must've been attracted to her."

"Not like that. Not at first. We went to Bangkok together shortly after we met. Maybe I was deluding myself, but after living with men for so long, I wanted to hear a feminine voice, touch a woman's soft skin, hell, I guess I just needed to feel important to somebody."

As if from a very great distance, I hear the clink of a neighbor's snow shovel on his drive, Sally's soft snoring, the cycling of the refrigerator. It seems incomprehensible that the world is going on as usual.

The words burst from me. "You were important to me. To Jenny."

Sam scrubs his face with his hands. "Don't you think I knew that? But you weren't there. Izzy, think about it. I wasn't sure I'd ever see my family again."

"You know, I'm not sure this is getting us anyplace. I thought I should hear, but—"

"We were intimate only a few times. Shortly before I met you in Honolulu."

It is as if he understands that despite my hurt, I need to know those very details. A half scoff, half sob escapes me. "Well, that explains it."

"What?"

"You were practically a stranger to me that week."

"Oh, God, Iz. I was eaten up with guilt. One glimpse of you and I knew I'd fouled up big-time. That I wasn't worthy of you." He rests his head on the sofa back, then sighs, before looking back at me. "I broke it off with Diane as soon as I returned to base."

"Not quite soon enough." I know he wants forgiveness, but in the moment, all I have to offer is sarcasm.

"Yeah. Not quite soon enough. Iz, you've got to believe me. I never knew she was pregnant."

"That was convenient. What do you suppose you would've done had you known?"

"I'd never have left you and Jenny."

In my heart, I know that's the truth. But it's cold comfort right now.

"I guess we both owe Diane a debt of gratitude," Sam says quietly.

"I wonder if Mark would agree with you."

"We'll never know."

That does it. "Are you insane? I'm ripped to shreds by what has happened, but I have no understanding whatsoever how you can say such a thing. The man is searching for his family. And we are it. Diane may have done you a favor, but she didn't do her son one. My God, Sam, he needs to know his father. Like it or not, that's you."

Then, blinded by rage, I grab his arm and pull him into the kitchen, where I turn up the volume on the phone and play Mark's message. The color drains from Sam's face, and in the awful silence that follows, I can hear his teeth grinding. "Like it or not, you have a son. He has a voice. He is real. Now deal with it."

I whirl from the room and pick up my journal before turning back to my stunned husband. "Now, if you'll excuse me, I'm going to the bedroom. By myself. Fix yourself a peanut butter sandwich for lunch."

Seething, I remain in control until I reach our room where I fling myself down beside Orville and give way to the sobs I've held in check throughout our painful conversation. Six tissues later, I pull up the comforter, exhausted.

I'm awakened by a tap on the door. When I open it, no one is there. On the floor is a tray with a grilled-cheese sandwich and a steaming pot of tea. In memory I hear my mother's voice. *Isabel, a pot of tea will fix anything.*

I wish I could believe her.

Glancing at the tray, I realize I'm ravenous. The

sandwich is surprisingly good, but it fails as a peace offering. Until Sam can talk about Mark Taylor and we can agree on a course of action, we are at a stalemate.

The phone rings, and I grab the receiver. Lisa starts abruptly. "When is Daddy coming to fix the dishwasher?"

"He just got home last night."

"I know. I talked to him yesterday. He said he'd come as soon as the roads were clear."

"I'll put your father on. But before I do, how's my grandson?"

"Just fine. He's out sledding with the neighborhood kids."

"And how are you?"

"Actually, I'm having some fun. I've had a few dates with a man I met through a friend at work. An older man." She hesitates and her voice softens. "I hope you'll approve."

"Is he someone special?" I hold my breath. If Lisa's not in the mood to confide, I will get nothing.

"I don't know yet, but I think he could be and it's scary."

"It can't be easy starting to date again. What's Scooter's reaction?"

"He's pretty used to being the alpha male."

"He's an important part of the equation. For both your sakes, take it slow and easy."

"Jeez, Mom, you sound like Dear Abby."

"Okay, okay. I'll quit the motherly thing."

"So can I speak to Daddy?"

"Most certainly." I holler at Sam, who picks up in the kitchen. Before I click off, I hear Lisa's butter-wouldn't-melt-in-her-mouth comment. "Remember, Daddy, you promised."

I go into the bathroom, scrub my face and reapply makeup. Sooner or later, I have to face my husband again. It may as well be now. As I walk down the hall to the family room, Sally runs toward me. She really is a nice dog and I appreciate her affection. I kneel and murmur sweet nothings in her ear as I scratch her back.

Sam's waiting by the window in the family room. The sun is now obscured by clouds and a wind moans around the house. "More snow is forecast," he says. "Unusual for this time of year."

"Thank you for the sandwich."

He turns around. "You're welcome." He walks to me, then pulls me against his chest, where I inhale the familiar, comforting scent of him. "I'm so sorry to put you through all of this."

I can't help myself and snuggle into the softness of his flannel shirt. "I'm sorry, too. But painful as it is, we're not done talking yet."

"Can it wait?"

I wish we could postpone it forever. "Not for

long, but maybe we've both had enough for one day." I stand back. "What about Lisa? Won't you be going there tomorrow?"

"I told her she could hang on a bit longer or call a repairman. You're more important right now."

Ordinarily, I would urge Sam to go to Boulder to help his daughter, but this time I'm glad he's put me first.

FOR THE REST OF THE afternoon we move into domestic mode, a routine that temporarily defuses the situation. I put in a load of wash and Sam heads for the grocery store with my list. The house yawns with emptiness, not just because Sam is physically gone, but because the psychological distance between us is so great. I have a sudden urge to talk to Twink, who always tells me what I need to hear.

Curling up in my special chair, I dial her New York number and in two rings hear her breezy voice. "Isabel Irene Lambert, I'd about given up on you. When I saw your name on the Caller ID, I said to myself, 'Aha. About time.'"

"Well, hello to you, too." Hearing her voice makes me smile for the first time in days. "What do you mean 'about time'?"

"Do you have any idea how transparent you are? When we spoke last, I sensed something was wrong. But I know you. You don't tell me a thing until you're ready."

"How's a girl supposed to keep any secrets?"

"You're not. At least not from someone who's seen you with stains on your best bib and tucker and heard you say how icky Laidslaw Barton Grosbeak's kisses were."

I can't help it, I laugh out loud. "Sometimes I wish you didn't have such a long memory. I can't believe you remembered his entire name."

"Some things you never forget."

"Pardon the insensitive segue, but speaking of forgetting, how's your mother?"

"Her new medication helps some, but it's still a grim scenario."

"I'm sorry, Twink."

"Me, too." Following a beat of silence, she says, "Nice try, Lambert, but you're not going to sidetrack me that easily. What's going on with you?"

I don't even know where to start, only that I must. "Ever read those Victorian novels?"

"Now there's a non sequitur if I ever heard one."

"You know, where the hero wanders around the countryside and then comes to the house where the portly squire says, 'Welcome home, son. You were kidnapped at birth and we've hunted everywhere for you.'"

"Oh, like *Oliver* and *Tom Jones?*"

"Exactly."

"So?"

"About ten days ago, I was home alone minding my own business, when a young man knocked on the door and said, 'I'm your long-lost son.' Well, not mine, but Sam's."

"Excuse me?"

"My reaction exactly. It seems Sam had an affair with an air force nurse while he was serving in Thailand."

"Sam? You're kidding."

"No, I'm not."

"Jeez, that was a stupid thing to say. Of course you wouldn't kid about something like that. I have a million questions, but first, how are you?"

"I'm not sure. I'm hurt…and angry that we wasted so much time not being honest after Blake's death and Sam's return from Southeast Asia. I knew our marriage was different from before. At the time, it seemed, well, normal. Lots of military marriages suffered in those days. I thought that I could suck it up and go on."

"And you did."

"But, boy, when the cracks opened up, they were huge."

"How can I help?"

"You can administer a heaping dose of reality." I take a deep breath and tell her about Mark

Taylor, Diane Berrigan and Sam's unwillingness to deal with his son.

"Izzy, can you accept this young man into your life?"

"It's not his fault, Twink. Jenny and Lisa have a half brother. Is it fair for me—or Sam for that matter—to keep that knowledge from them? Or to deny Mark answers he has a right to know? Sure, it presents problems, but I met him, Twink. He looks like Sam, he even has some of his mannerisms. His mother died recently. In all those years, she never revealed Sam's identity. Now that Mark has made his way to Sam, he refuses to see him."

"Does he give a reason?"

"No, but he's adamant."

"He'll come around in time."

"I'm sick and tired of Sam Lambert's delayed time schedule."

"Do you have a choice?"

"I don't know. All I do know is that this isn't the way things ought to be." With sudden clarity, I know exactly where those words came from. I turn and glare at the billiken, who eyes me from his Olympian perch.

"Izzy, you've always wanted the picture-perfect life, the one your mother laid out for you. In a monumental act of defiance, you married Sam. You were crazy, madly in love with him. You still

are. Your whirlwind courtship was the stuff of
romance novels. Your grandmother groomed you
for fairy-tale endings." She hesitates. "It ain't
happenin,' Miss Isabel."

I swallow hard. As usual, Twink is right on
target. "You're telling me I'm in la-la land?"

"Not la-la land, fantasyland. What made you
think Sam was perfect or that your life would sail
along smoothly without problems?"

"Are you forgetting Blake?"

"Oh, honey, never. That's not what I'm talking
about. When Sam returned from overseas, I saw
the effort you made to create a storybook
marriage. You outdid June Cleaver, Donna Reed
and that Brady woman, whatever her name was,
all rolled into one. And it worked."

"But you saw chinks?"

"Only because I know you so well."

"It's not working now."

"But it will, Izzy, it will. Sam adores you. I
used to long for just one week with a man who
would look at me the way he looks at you."

"He's infuriating."

"Give it up. You love him. And, ta-dah, guess
what? He's flawed."

My heart stirs at her words. I do love Sam.

"Do you need me to come?"

Twink has been there for me through the births

of my children and the death of my son, but the situation with my husband is my own to handle. "Thanks for offering, but, no. This is between Sam and me."

"Good girl. I love you, you know."

"I count on that. Me, too, you."

After we hang up, I sit in the gathering dusk. Finally, I look up and give a grudging nod of understanding to the billiken.

SAM AND I WATCH THE news and learn more snow is forecast. When he goes to bed, I stay in the family room, appreciating the quiet. It wasn't easy hearing Twink's perception of my marriage, even as it rang true. I *had* thought if I hosted enough parties, networked with Sam's fellow officers' wives, reared well-behaved children and kept an immaculate home that it would be enough. For his part, Sam provided well for his family, took us interesting places, lavished gifts on "his girls" at Christmas and on birthdays. In comparison with Twink's life, mine has been blessed.

With my friend's words fresh in my mind, I pick up my journal, convinced that what I am writing is more therapy than memoir. The girls won't benefit from my candor. When this is all over, I'll prepare a gentler account for them.

Post-Vietnam years

FROM THE MOMENT SAM returned from Southeast Asia, it was as if we'd entered into an unspoken agreement to fashion a new, different kind of marriage. I dismissed his reticence as a natural consequence of the war and learned that his readjustment required of me a corresponding readjustment of expectations.

The routine of military life, with its clear rules and regimented order, formed the boundaries of our days. Within that framework, Sam and I gradually relaxed into a relationship that worked for us. I was the children's disciplinarian and the domestic field marshal, he was the adored daddy and solid, attentive husband.

Looking back, I have to say that I really thought we were happy. We had charming daughters and enjoyed many good times. Certainly, I never felt neglected. Yet in those post-Vietnam years, some elusive spark was missing from our relationship. I rationalized that, over the course of time, most marriages were like that, my parents being a prime example. I told myself it was romantic nonsense to pine for the Sam Lambert who'd lived to fly, stormed Springbranch and carried me off to an Arkansas judge.

Generally life went smoothly until Sam's retirement from the military in 1989. By some standards, we had lived a glamorous life, with postings in Alaska, England and Washington, D.C., among others. He was accustomed to being in command and to the camaraderie of his fellow officers. Our civilian life began in Colorado Springs, which made sense. The state was home to him, and the perks available to military retirees in that area were significant.

What should have been one of the best chapters of our lives was not. I vividly remember the evening in the late summer of 1990 when Sam came home from his evening jog and sank onto the glider on our front porch with its panoramic view of Pike's Peak. "I've had it, Izzy. Shit. How many rounds of golf can I play? I'm useless."

It was one of those times I knew to keep my mouth shut.

"What am I supposed to do? Join a friggin' garden club? Play shuffleboard with those old geezers in Acacia Park?" He must have sensed I was going to say something, because he cut me off. "Stop. I don't want to hear how I should volunteer for some nonprofit organization or tutor kids at the grade school."

I let him rant. Finally, I said, "I don't suppose it would help to tell you you're not useless, that you've earned this retirement."

He leaned forward, hands on his knees. "Hell, I feel like a dinosaur."

A week later he found me in the kitchen after breakfast. "What would you say if I went back to work?"

"Work? What are you talking about?"

"I can't just sit around, Iz. A few weeks ago I met a retired colonel at the Air Force Academy Golf Course. He owns a big development company and needs some help. Asked me if I'd be interested in trying my hand at sales."

The rest is history. Sam thrived on the action and enjoyed befriending his clients, many of them fellow military men.

At that same time, my life changed dramatically, too. My mother's health began to deteriorate. When she could no longer live alone, we moved her from Springbranch to a Colorado residential facility. Until she died in 1991, my days were occupied with visits and her doctors' appointments.

After her death, I began to do those things I had suggested to Sam—volunteer at the branch library, tutor at the grade school and work in our garden. We had a host of friends, enjoyed frequent travels and adored being close to Jenny, Lisa and the grandchildren.

When Sam retired for the final time, after having made a great deal of money, we were able to build this house, each detail so lovingly planned. Moving to Breckenridge and fulfilling Sam's dream gave us both tremendous satisfaction.

I thought life couldn't get much better. Never in my wildest dreams did I think it would get so much worse. In my *Better Homes and Gardens* world, I deluded myself that things were exactly as they ought to be.

CHAPTER TEN

Breckenridge, Colorado

SAM STOOD IN THE DARKNESS, gazing out the bedroom window, mesmerized by the falling snowflakes suspended in the glow of the yard light. As he'd feared, the nightmares had come, prompted by yesterday's conversation that had brought the war back with gut-wrenching immediacy. Until Izzy had come to bed, he'd tossed and turned. Even then he'd lain awake for another hour.

Suddenly, without warning, he was in a whining nosedive, shoulder straps cutting into his flesh, his face plastered against his cheek bone, playing a desperate game of tag with missiles and Vietcong fighters. Fireworks erupted all around him. Pulling out just above the treetops, he streaked toward the heavens, pursued by a multiplying number of enemy planes. In his headphones screeched ear-splitting static punctuated by the oaths and obscenities of his wingman. In that flying coffin, his breath came in pants, sweat clouded his eyes and the panicked scream he heard above it all was his own.

He'd jerked awake, gasping for breath, perspiring under the comforter, his heart hammering. When he'd thrown back the covers and gone to get a drink, shivers racked him. He'd been standing at the window ever since.

Minutes passed as more snow piled up. Knowing further sleep was impossible, Sam went to his upstairs study where he pulled a tattered photo album from the bookcase and settled at his desk. Although he had not opened this particular album in years, something compelled him now. There they were—the twenty-four pilots of his original Udorn squadron members—hats shoved back, arms draped around one another, grins cocky. He forced himself to name those he could remember. Twenty had come home, two of those from a Vietcong prison camp.

Then he did what he had never done since returning from Southeast Asia. From the inside lining of the cover where he'd hidden it, he withdrew a faded black-and-white photograph. Beside a Thai flower vendor stood an air force captain, his arm encircling a willowy blonde holding a huge bouquet of lilies. Even squinting, he could not bring the two strangers into focus.

Who were these people? The relationship seemed illusory, as if it had never happened. But it had. The proof of it had knocked on the door and rocked his world.

Deliberately, he tore the picture of himself and Diane into fourths, then fed it to the paper shredder. Keeping the photograph would be the final insult to Izzy.

But a son? His gut churned when he thought about the man.

Even though Sam hadn't seen him, what he visualized was an adult with Blake's trusting baby face.

An hour later Izzy tapped him on the shoulder. "Sam, honey, come back to bed." He'd fallen asleep at his desk, head cradled in his arms. "Restless night?"

Groggily he stared up at her. She was always beautiful even first thing in the morning without makeup. "Too much on my mind."

She pulled her robe closer. "Humor me. Try to rest."

To his amazement he awakened three hours later, refreshed.

AFTER A LATE BREAKFAST, the snow lightened to an occasional flurry. Overnight an additional four inches had accumulated. Now the sun was shining, and the higher temperatures and brisk wind would soon melt the covering on the driveway. Izzy sat across the table and got right to the point.

"You heard Mark Taylor on the answering machine yesterday. He's been remarkably patient."

Instantly irritated, Sam grunted in response.

"When he left here, I told him to go home and give us some time. I promised we would get back to him after you decided whether to meet him. It's been nearly two weeks, Sam. We owe him an answer."

"My answer is to ask him to leave us alone." Ignoring Izzy's look of disbelief, he continued. "Do you realize how devastating this could be to our family? Would Jenny and Lisa appreciate knowing their father was an adulterer? That a stranger wants to call himself their half brother? Somebody has to think about our girls, and it doesn't seem to be you. You're ready to throw a welcome-home party for a stranger. Well, I'm not." His face turned red. "Next thing you know, he'll expect to be written into the will."

Izzy stood, forcefully shoving her chair under the table. "My God, Sam, listen to what you're saying. You got yourself into this mess and now you want to pretend it never happened. Well, it did, and I'm not going to be the one to tell that young man that you're utterly indifferent to him."

"Even if I am?"

"No matter how many times you delude yourself with that rhetoric, I know you better." She leaned into his face. "We have a problem, Sam. And you are not going to run. You are not going to hide. You are going to face it." She crossed to the phone and picked up the receiver. "I'm calling Mark Taylor now. What I'd like to tell him is that his long-lost father is heartless. But I won't do that. I will tell him you are still weighing the options and ask for his continued patience and understanding. And when I hang up, you and I are going to deal with this once and for all."

Izzy was deaf to his objections. She would do what she wanted anyway. Sam left the room. He had no desire to overhear her conversation.

He was baffled. Why was she so eager for him to meet Mark? He wasn't her son. Worse yet, each time she looked at him, he would remind her of Sam's infidelity. Sam stomped up the stairs and barricaded himself in his office.

HE PAID BILLS AND recorded stock transactions, perversely thankful for the busywork insulating him from Izzy's demands. As far as he was concerned, they were at a stalemate and further discussion was useless and emotionally draining.

When the phone rang, he glared at it. He'd let

Izzy answer. It might be Mark Taylor returning her call. Fuming, he stared at the computer screen.

"Sam! Come quick." There was urgency in his wife's voice. "Hurry," she screamed. He met her at the foot of the stairs. Her face was drained of color and her hands shook. She sank onto the steps. "It's Scooter. Oh, God, Sam, it's our Scooter." She thrust the phone at him. "Talk to Lisa."

"Honey, what is it?"

"Oh, Daddy, it's…it's Scooter. He's been—"

"Calm down, Lisa. Take a deep breath. Now tell me what happened."

"We're at the emergency room. He…he…was sledding again this morning and there was this tree and…he's unconscious and, oh, Daddy, I'm so scared."

Izzy's eyes swam with worry. As they had always done in the cockpit, Sam's instincts kicked into autopilot. "What are his injuries?"

"I…I don't know yet. The EMTs said something about a concussion and possible internal injuries, maybe broken ribs and a punctured lung, but the ER doctors aren't telling me anything yet. I need you, Daddy. Come quick."

"We'll leave right now. What hospital?… Boulder?… Okay, we'll be there as soon as we can. If anything changes, you have our cell numbers." Then an unpleasant thought occurred to him. The boy's father needed to be notified. "Have you called Neal?"

"Do I have to?"

She sounded like a little girl. "You know you do." Even as he said the words, he could anticipate the tension that would result from Neal's being in the same room. Their divorce had turned nasty over custody of Scooter, although Sam had suspected Neal was more interested in wielding control over Lisa than in rearing his son. "Listen to me, sweetheart. It's normal to be scared. But Scooter is getting expert treatment."

By the time they concluded their conversation, Lisa's sobs had subsided and Izzy had brushed past him to retrieve their suitcases from the storage closet.

After hanging up, Sam paused momentarily, dread washing over him. Izzy held out the phone book. "Could you call the kennel and see if we can board Orville and Sally and ask the neighbors to pick up our mail and papers?"

While she was in full prep mode, he was having an intense delayed reaction. Lisa was counting on her daddy to fix everything. She should've known better.

WITHIN THE HOUR, they dropped off the animals and set out for Boulder. United in their concern, he and Izzy had temporarily set aside their differences. In fact, he'd even asked whether she'd reached Mark Taylor.

"Yes," she replied. "He was disappointed but he's agreed to give you more time."

That was all they said on the subject. Before leaving, Izzy had called Jenny to tell her about Scooter. During their drive, Izzy punctuated the silence with conjectures. "What if Scooter's in a coma?" "Maybe he should be moved to Children's Hospital in Denver." "A punctured lung could be serious."

Sam let her talk. At least she didn't seem to require answers from him. Although he tried to concentrate on his driving, he was worried sick. The miles dragged by until finally they reached the hospital.

Bursting through the emergency room door, they scanned the waiting room. No Lisa. At the desk they learned Scooter had been transferred to pediatric ICU. Izzy clutched Sam's hand as they entered the elevator, joining two scrub-suited women and a harried-looking young man. No one spoke. Arriving at their floor, they read the directional signs and took off at a run, stopping finally at the nursing station. "We're Samuel Creighton's grandparents. Scooter's."

The nurse pointed to a waiting room at the end

of the hall. "You can't see your grandson now, but your family is in the waiting area."

When Lisa spotted them, she threw herself into her father's arms. "Thank God, you're both here." Over her shoulder, Sam spotted Neal, his lips set in a grim line, avoiding Sam's glance. When Lisa turned to hug Izzy, she broke down. "Mom, it's all my fault." She wiped at her tears. "I shouldn't have let him go sledding."

"Honey, easy. Boys will be boys. It's not your fault." Izzy and Sam led her toward chairs some distance from Neal. "What have the doctors said?"

She sniffled into a tissue then sank into a chair. "He's still unconscious. They've taken him for a cranial CT scan and chest X-rays. Oh, Mom, he's so little. He just lies there, with his eyes closed. So still. And his breathing scares me. It's awful." She hugged herself against the spasms racking her body.

Izzy picked up Lisa's hand. "He'll come out of it. It takes time. And, you know, a punctured lung can heal itself."

Neal came over to where the three were sitting. It was all Sam could do not to coldcock the two-timing bastard. Then he winced. *Who the hell am I to judge him?*

Neal looked from Izzy to Sam. "Sorry to see you folks under these circumstances." Then he turned to Lisa. "I'll be back later."

"You're leaving? We don't have the scan results yet." She stared at her ex-husband without comprehension.

"I have an engagement."

"One that's more important than our son?"

"Of course not, but what am I accomplishing sitting here?"

Lisa shrugged in a show of indifference. "Not a thing, Neal. Go on. Scooter and I can do without you just fine. We've had lots of practice."

Neal stuffed his hands into his pockets, nervously jingling his keys and coins. "You have my cell number. Call me if there's any change. I'll be back later." Then he turned and strode down the hall.

Lisa shook her head. "Unbelievable." Then she glanced at the wall clock over the coffee bar. "It's taking too long." She got up and retrieved her purse from where she was sitting before they arrived. "I need to call Jenny."

"We've done that," Izzy said. "When Don gets home from work with the four-wheel drive, she'll be on her way."

That news brought a fresh round of tears. "I'm so scared."

"Of course, you are. And waiting is difficult. But you need to keep up your strength for Scooter. Have you eaten?"

"I'm not hungry."

"You need to eat." Izzy shot him a look, and he knew he'd received his marching orders.

"I'm on my way."

"No more yucky black coffee, please," Lisa said. "See if they have cappuccino."

"Me, too," Izzy added.

Back in the lobby, he consulted the hospital floor plan and headed for the cafeteria where he settled on a chicken salad sandwich and chips. Yet even as he poured two cappuccinos, he knew Lisa would barely nibble on the food. Ashamedly, he realized he was delaying his return to Lisa and Izzy, as if loitering there would postpone bad news. Izzy's accusations hit him. *This is always the way you handle trouble. You run, Sam, you run.*

God help him, maybe that was what he was doing. Everything about a hospital set his nerves on edge. The clinical detachment of the nurses and doctors brushing past the poor schmucks who relied on them for some crumb of information and hope. The rattles and pings of mechanical devices with purposes unknown to the lay person. The futility of the unanswered blinking light above a patient's door. He stuffed the food and drinks into a cardboard carrier and returned to the pediatric unit.

Izzy was alone in the waiting room. She stood when he came in. He held out the food. "Where's Lisa?"

"With Scooter. They just brought him back from his CT scan and X-ray."

He handed Izzy a cappuccino and set the carrier on the lamp table.

"I didn't want to say this in front of Lisa, but Scooter's been out for several hours." She took a sip of her drink. "What if something—"

"Don't go there, Iz. We have to think positive."

They sat quietly while she drank her cappucino. "Can you believe Neal?"

"Oh, yeah." He recalled how he'd always thought Neal was too slick, too smooth. "He's the same self-absorbed prick."

A fleeting smile teased Izzy's lips. "Why don't you tell it like it is, dear?"

"The jerk hurt our daughter badly."

"Lisa told me she's seeing someone. An older fellow with grown children."

He summoned humor to mask the unsettled feeling in his stomach. "Can he repair a dishwasher?"

"Sam!"

"Just trying to find the silver lining."

Izzy patted his knee. "Be fair."

Sam grimaced. "I just want her to be happy." He paced to the window, which overlooked the parking lot. In the hallway an orderly called out, "Colorado's ahead, 21-7." At the moment, that was the most inconsequential information Sam had ever heard.

"Dad? Mom?" Lisa stood in the doorway beckoning. "The nurse says you can come in with me."

He picked up the food carton, and followed his wife and daughter into a darkened room where they surrounded the bed. Lisa caressed her son's arm. Scooter's forehead was swollen and discolored, and his mouth and nose were concealed behind an oxygen mask. The rhythmic click of a monitor and the rise and fall of Scooter's chest were all that convinced Sam he was alive. "Scooter, honey, it's Mom. Can you hear me? Please wake up." Lisa gazed at the ceiling, as if searching for magical words. "The Colorado football game's on. You don't want to miss that."

Sam set the food on the counter and pushed the lone chair closer, so Lisa could sit. Izzy stood behind Lisa, her hands on Lisa's shoulder. Minutes passed. The air was suffocating. He was about to step into the hall when a young man in a white coat, a stethoscope draped around his neck, bustled into the room.

"Mrs. Creighton?" Lisa nodded. "I'm Dr. Finley." He looked at Sam and Izzy. "You must be Scooter's grandparents. I'm the pediatric resident on call. I've just reviewed the boy's CT scan and X-ray. At the moment, it would appear there is no intracranial bleeding. That's a good thing. But the sooner he regains consciousness the better. It will help if one of you is with him at all times. If you can talk to him, sing, play the radio, anything that might stimulate his brain, that may help."

"And if he doesn't come to soon…?"

"Let's not cross that bridge yet. His vitals are good. I'm hoping for the best."

Easy for you to say, Sam thought, then chided himself for his pettiness.

"The X-rays show two broken ribs, one of which punctured his right lung. We're hopeful that the collapsed lung will repair itself, but we're monitoring him carefully and if we need to insert a chest tube, we will. Meanwhile, we'll be moving him into a larger room nearer the nurses' station. Those surroundings will be more comfortable for you. And, Mrs. Creighton, we encourage you to spend the night here with him."

Lisa nodded. "Thank you."

Shortly after the doctor left, a nurse and an orderly arrived with a gurney to move Scooter. Sam excused himself, loath to watch them move the still body, tethered to an oxygen tank and an IV stand. He went to an area where cell phone usage was permitted and called Jenny to give her the latest update.

"I'm leaving within the hour, Dad, so I should be there no later than nine. How's Lisa?"

"A wreck, as you might expect."

"Aren't we all?"

"Yes," he said in classic understatement. "Have a safe trip. Lisa will be relieved to have you here."

He was drawn to Scooter's room even as his footsteps dragged. He felt completely inadequate.

Izzy joined him at the foot of the bed, slipping her arm around his waist. Lisa sat on a chair positioned near Scooter's head crooning an old Beatles' tune.

"He's so still," Sam observed. "Poor little guy."

"Lisa and I have been talking. She needs some clothes and toiletries if she's going to spend the night. Could you stay with Scooter while I run her home? That way I can gather some things for Scooter while she packs her things."

It was one way he could help. "Sure. You go along."

"Mom, I don't know if I should leave. What if he…"

"We'll only be gone a short time and your father will be here."

Slowly, Lisa rose to her feet, her eyes never leaving her son. "Okay, I guess. If Daddy's staying."

Izzy led her toward the door, where Sam folded her in his arms. "I'll be right beside him."

"We'll hurry," Izzy said by way of encouraging Lisa to step into the hall.

"But—" She looked over her shoulder at the figure in the bed.

"Go ahead. He'll be fine." Sam prayed he was telling the truth.

The last thing he heard Lisa say as they moved down the hall was "I need to call Neal, don't I?"

"Son of a bitch," he muttered as he took the chair Lisa had vacated.

It was several minutes before he noticed the cardboard container. Lisa hadn't eaten. No wonder. He wasn't hungry, either.

TALK TO HIM, THE doctor had said. Sam didn't know where to begin, but he started in anyway. "When I was a boy, there wasn't much of any place to go sledding. The country was flat as a pancake. Sometimes, after a snow, the older boys would tie ropes to car bumpers and drag us around on sleds or trash can lids. I suppose it was dangerous, but at the time, we thought it was fun."

Goddamn it, kid. Are ya tryin' to kill yourself? Then his father's derisive laugh. *Who'd do the dishes, then?*

"Yeah, fun. Well, another time a bunch of us guys loaded some hogs into a couple of pickups and let them loose in the high school principal's yard. The next morning there was pig shit everywhere. On Monday, Old Man Neggers kept the whole school in after the dismissal bell rang. Said he wouldn't let us go until someone confessed. But none of us guys said a word. Finally, when parents began calling asking where their kids were, he let us go. But I'll tell you one thing—he didn't shake my hand at graduation."

A nurse opened the door and sidled alongside the bed. "Just checking his vitals," she said. He watched her place the blood pressure cuff and take Scooter's pulse. When she finished, she smiled. "No change. Can I bring you anything?"

"No, thanks, I'm fine." *Fine? What a crock!* She left, closing the door quietly behind her.

He searched for another topic. For some perverse reason, Neal came to mind. "Hey, little guy, it's a funny thing about fathers. You never know what sort you're going to get. Some are great. They take you to ball games, rig up a tire swing in the backyard so you can throw perfect passes, teach you about building fires and pitching tents.

"But they're not all that way. Take mine, for instance. I barely remember him before my mama got so sick. Only a few things. He taught me how to ride a bike and one summer he drove us all into Denver to the amusement park. I think he even laughed. But I can't say for sure, because after she died, it was like he was always angry. Lloyd and

I were nuisances he had to put up with. I couldn't wait until I was grown and could leave home."

He readjusted his chair so he could watch the monitor. "It's gotta be tough for you with your parents divorced. I hope your dad is the kind I mentioned before. One who'll take you camping. Teach you to fish. Regardless of what goes on with him, though, I'm here for you, buddy."

Sam fell silent, wondering how Lisa and Neal's divorce had affected their son. There was so much he didn't know, hadn't asked.

The bruised little face on the pillow wrenched his heart. Gently he brushed a lock of blond hair off the boy's forehead. Reaching for his hand, Sam willed it to respond, but it rested limply in his. The sound of labored breathing filled the silence.

He was at a loss for words, helpless to know how to penetrate the depths of his grandson's consciousness. Then, from out of nowhere, the song came, and he began to sing. "Off we go into the wild blue yonder…"

A roll call of those who went "down in flame" thundered in his chest. The quiet of the hospital room came alive with the cacophony of antiaircraft fire and the drone of a hundred engines. His words died out with "…nothing can stop the U.S. Air Force."

He pulled the blanket closer around Scooter's

shoulders. "Son, I don't know what to tell you about war. Throughout history, it's what men have always done. Make no mistake, there's a thrill to it. I loved climbing into the cockpit of that million-dollar aircraft. When I'd lift off and soar to the heights, I felt like the king of the world, limited only by the heavens. That's the good part.

"Some of the best men I ever met didn't come home. They went down with their planes or bailed out over dense jungle where Vietcong waited. That's the bad part.

"You know what I want for you, son? For you to grow up strong and sure. To find a passion, something you love to do. And if it's the air force, I'd be proud, but…but…" His throat constricted and he couldn't speak.

Bile filled his throat. Suddenly he was seeing another boy, an infant, who'd never had a chance. He gripped the blanket between his fists and strangled on the name. "Blake! My God, Blake!"

The body in front of him wasn't Blake's, and on some level he knew that. But the words, the words he'd been saying…those were the words he'd whispered to his son when he lay beside him in the hammock, when he'd rocked him in his arms after his bath and Blake had smelled all powdery and new. His gut ripped in two. He couldn't catch his breath. Something wet covered his face and he felt caged, like a wild beast. "Blake!" Did he cry the name out loud? He couldn't move, but neither could he stay. Panic, like none he'd ever known, consumed him.

In a split second of clarity, he buzzed for the nurse before rushing from the room and racing down the hall. The air was dense and a jangle of voices and noises assailed him. He ran, faster and faster. Finding the stairway, he hurtled downward toward fresh air. In the lobby, blinded, he bolted for the door and the cold night air. He couldn't stop even then. He darted through the cars in the parking lot and out onto a sidewalk leading to a strip mall. His breaths came in gasps and cold air filled his lungs. But still he ran.

Until he collapsed on the bench of a bus stop shelter. Only then did he realize that his own tears were blinding him. And that the pain in his gut had a name. Blake. Then he howled at the immovable mountains. "Blake!"

He had no understanding of how he could go on. Scooter was the reincarnation of his son. And just like before, he could do friggin', goddamned nothing to help the child.

CHAPTER ELEVEN

Boulder, Colorado

LISA AND I DRIVE OUT OF the hospital lot and she phones Neal with the doctor's report. I hear her say, "Whatever. You're only his father." After shutting off her phone, she stares out the passenger window, preoccupied. Finally she looks up. "Mom, I don't understand the man. He made such a show of wanting custody of Scooter, but now he sees no reason to come to the hospital until morning. I'm to contact him if something goes wrong."

I refrain from offering my opinion.

"In a way I'm glad. Neal makes me nervous. At the moment, Scooter won't know he's not there. Funny, though, wild horses couldn't keep me away."

"Some men can't deal with illness and hospitals."

"But Daddy's there. He's not flaking out on us."

I have no answer for her.

At Lisa's house, I persuade her to eat some

chicken noodle soup before she starts gathering her things. In Scooter's bedroom I find a small athletic bag with a Denver Broncos logo. I pack his robe and slippers, some Spider-Man briefs, socks, sneakers, a University of Colorado sweatshirt and a pair of jeans. After zipping the bag shut, I glance around. Posters of football and basketball players hang on one wall, framed photos of Scooter on another. In the corner is a pile of books, puzzles and toy trucks and planes. I swallow hard, pick up the bag and join Lisa in the kitchen. Unexpectedly she hesitates in the doorway. "I'd like to call Hank."

"Hank?"

A faint flush colors her cheeks. "The man I've been dating."

"This sounds more serious than you've let on."

"Maybe. I, mean, I hope. Jenny thinks he's too old for me."

"What do you think?"

"I don't know, Mom. Only that I need him right now." She looks like a child asking permission to dive off the high board.

"Then call him."

To give her some privacy, I slip down the hall to the powder room. When I return, she's ready to leave. "I caught him at the gym where he works out. He's going home to shower and change before coming to the hospital." She looks beyond me to study the portrait of Scooter over the piano. "I'm sorry. I didn't want you to meet Hank like this."

"Now seems like a pretty good time." As I say it, I realize it's true. The fact that she's turned to this man in a crisis is proof that he's become important to her.

It is a crisp evening, one of those cloudless nights when it seems as if the moon and stars are at one's fingertips. As we drive along, it's evident that Boulder is partying following the big Colorado University football victory. Restaurants and bars are packed, and revelers wander the street. The incongruity strikes me. They are celebrating while we can only worry.

Lisa hurries from the parking lot to the elevators, where we catch a car on the way up. Approaching the pediatric unit, I sense her growing tension.

As she tears down the hall toward Scooter's room, a nurse follows us. "Mrs. Creighton?"

Lisa stops. "What is it?"

Catching up to us, the nurse leads us to an empty room. "Before you see your son, there's something I need to tell you."

"Oh, God." Lisa sags against me.

"Oh, no, it's not your son. It's about your father."

In that instant, I know. Sam has run again.

"About ten minutes ago, your father rang for a

nurse, and then rushed down the hall and out of the building. From the window of the nurses' station, I saw him dash through the parking lot and down the street. I hope nothing's wrong, but I didn't want you to be startled when you go into the room. One of our staff has been sitting with Scooter since he left."

"Mom?" Lisa stares at me, as if I have the answer. "Why would he leave Scooter?"

"I'm not sure, honey." I thank the nurse and then walk Lisa toward Scooter's room. "I'll get you settled and then look for him."

"Where would he go?"

I have no earthly idea but I say, "Maybe he needed some air. There's a Starbucks nearby. He's probably having coffee, reading the newspaper." Even as I say it, I know it's not true. "After all, he did ring for the nurse."

"But he promised to stay," she reminds me.

"I know." I cannot look at the expression of betrayal in her eyes.

In the room, nothing has changed. Lisa shrugs out of her coat and takes up her post at Scooter's side. Seeing the cafeteria food on the counter, I throw the sandwich and the container away, saving the chips in case Lisa gets hungry later. I force myself to move deliberately although every muscle in my body is coiled to race after Sam. My heart sinks when I spot his jacket slung on the dresser top. Why wouldn't he have put it on?

"And then Mamaw and I had some hot soup. The kind you like." Much of what Lisa is saying doesn't register. Where the hell is Sam? What would make him leave his grandson?

"Aunt Jenny will be here soon. I know she'd like you to wake up so she can say hello. Can you do that?"

I move closer to the bed. "Lisa, I have to try to find your father."

"Go, Mom. I'm worried about him, too."

"I'll be back soon," I say with false optimism. I pick up my purse and am moving toward the door when I hear a faint sound. I spin around.

Lisa is on her feet, her face inches from Scooter's. "What's that, Scooter?"

"Mom?" The boy's eyelids flutter. "It hurts."

Lisa motions for me to get a nurse. "Thank you, God," I murmur again and again as I locate Scooter's nurse and accompany her back to the room.

"Hey, little guy," she says, leaning over the bed and checking his pupils. "Welcome back. Did you have a comfy snooze?"

"Mom? Where are you?"

Lisa laughs with relief. "Right here, honey. I'm not going anywhere."

The nurse examines Scooter and readjusts his

oxygen mask. "I'll let the doctor know what's going on."

Sagging with relief, Lisa settles back in her chair and shakes her head in amazement. "We have so much to be thankful for. Now if his lung will just heal itself." Then, as if she's just remembered Sam, she waves her arm toward the door. "Go, Mom. Find Daddy. He'll want to know about Scooter."

I stop at the nurses' station to hear exactly where the nurse last saw Sam. She takes me to the window and indicates the direction he took. Then she lays a hand on my shoulder. "I didn't want to upset your daughter unnecessarily, but you should know your husband acted quite agitated, almost oblivious to his surroundings. We called out to him, but he ran right past us like a man possessed. Something must've upset him terribly. I had looked in the room a few minutes earlier, and he was calmly talking to his grandson. I have no explanation for what happened."

Alarm bells are going off in my head. "Neither do I. Thank you for the information."

When I reach the lobby, I can't decide whether to walk or to drive. Finally, I zip up my parka, pull on my mittens and start off across the parking lot and down the street.

Fifteen minutes later I am two blocks down the main artery combing the side streets. Starbucks is busy, but Sam isn't there. Half-drunken young men and giggly coeds look at me strangely when I peer into popular campus hangouts searching for him. I stop at a brightly lighted drugstore, hoping he's taken refuge there. No luck. With each dead end, I'm growing more frantic. What could have upset him so much? In desperation, I call the hospital, but I don't get the answer I'm hoping for. "I'm sorry, Mrs. Lambert. We haven't seen your husband since he left."

I cut across a convenience store parking lot and retrace my steps, knowing that before long, I will have to involve the police. Cars race up and down the street, black-and-gold university flags stuck to the windows, horns honking. I feel as if I'm moving in quicksand. The more I look, the more hopeless the search becomes. I walk on the other side of the main drag. There are fewer business establishments here, in the next block only a retaining wall and a lone bus stop shelter, but maybe from a different perspective, I'll see something I missed before.

As I approach the bus shelter, out of the corner of my eye, I catch a slight movement in the shadowy interior. I shudder. A mugger? What am I doing walking alone in the dark? Then I hear it. A pitiful moan. Then another. I move closer.

Inside a man sits on the bench, facing away from me, head bent, knees drawn up to his chest. "God, God."

I think my eyes are deceiving me, but they are not. It's Sam, unaware I'm here. Over and over, he repeats the unfinished prayer, his voice ragged.

So as not to alarm him, I call his name softly. Slowly he turns, studying me with unfocused eyes. Then I am in front of him, cupping his tear-stained face in my hands. "Sam, it's Izzy."

He encircles my waist and buries his head between my breasts. Then I feel it—the avalanche of emotion convulsing his body. His sobs tear the night and all I can do is stand and caress his hair, his heaving shoulders, his back. Wait for the spasm to pass.

After what seems like an eternity, his sobs subside and he stands and pulls me into a fierce embrace. "Izzy, my Izzy."

He feels cold, and I want to crawl inside him to warm him. "You're freezing," I whisper. I step back and gaze into his face. "Let's go, now." Everything in me wants to ask what has caused this breakdown, but instead I put my arm around him and lead him up the block and back to the parking lot. When we reach our car, I open the trunk lid and retrieve the old quilt I keep there for summer picnics. I hand it to him when I get into the car.

He wraps it around his shoulders. I crank up the heater and back out of the parking space. "Let's get you some hot coffee."

We head toward McDonald's without speaking. Sam is in some other world. I order, pull through the drive-thru and hand him the drink. It is then that he speaks. "Scooter?"

"He came to a little while ago."

"Thank God."

We return to the hospital lot. "Do you want to go in?"

"Not yet. I have some things I need to say."

"Okay, but first, I'll let Lisa know I've found you." I call the nurses' station and ask them to deliver the message. All the while I'm on the phone, he sits staring at his hands. That's when I notice the abrasions on his knuckles. "Sam?" I touch the back of one hand.

"I know. Pretty ugly."

"How…?"

His long sigh burdens my heart. "I took it out on the bus shelter. Why? It's a long story. A very long story."

"I'm listening. For as much time as it takes."

"It's—" his voice cracks "—Blake."

I'm stunned. I don't know what I expected, but not this. "Honey, that was decades ago."

He looks at me, his eyes haunted. "You think

I don't know that? Tonight it all came back, and for once I didn't have the resources to cram it back down into my gut." He shakes his head in bewilderment. "My God, I've never cried like that in my life."

"Maybe it was time."

"Iz, I was sitting there with Scooter. Everything was cool. I was telling him stories, just like the doc suggested, then I started singing the air force song and all these memories came back of guys we'd lost in 'Nam, and then I looked at Scooter, so helpless there, and I started talking to him just like I used to talk to Blake, and suddenly, hell, I lost it. Totally. I can't even describe the pain. So fierce I had to move, to outrun it, leave it far behind me. But the faster I ran, the worse it got, and all I could see in front of me was our little boy, who never even had a chance at life. And then there was Scooter and it all came together— Blake, Scooter, the war, my asshole of a father, the whole friggin' mess." He wipes his face. "Shit, Izzy, don't you understand? I couldn't do a thing about any of it."

I hesitate a few moments, then say, "Sam, you're not God."

"Well, if I were, I'd do a helluva lot better job."

"You don't mean that. Things happen. We're no more immune from trouble than the next folks."

He slumps in defeat. "You're right. I didn't mean that. It's just that, that…"

"That you're only now grieving. After all these years."

He looks up in disbelief. "I've grieved my whole life."

"Inside, where it ate you up every single day. There's nothing wrong with releasing your emotions."

"It's weak. I'm ashamed."

"Weak? Weak? It's the most manly thing you've ever done, my darling. Maybe now you can heal."

He takes a deep breath and his eyes fill again. "I never thought I could say any of this to you, Izzy."

I reach for his hand, careful to avoid the backs of his fingers. "Maybe that's where we got off track. I didn't help you get it out along the way. I grieved, too, but we never were able to share our pain. At the time, it just seemed easier for both of us to go along, holding it all in. But over the years, it's been a poison."

"I never wanted to let you down. To admit I was helpless."

"I know that."

"I love you, Isabel. You're the best thing that ever happened to me."

"It's simple. I love you, too."

"I know, and I'm grateful." He folds the quilt

and tosses it in the backseat. "What do you say? Let's go inside and see that grandson of ours. I think I need him as much as he needs me."

He puts his arm around me as we walk into the hospital, and when he smiles down at me, I melt. In his eyes is that same glint I saw on that long-ago Georgia night under a full moon. I was lost then, just as I am now over forty years later.

WHEN WE ENTER THE room, Scooter lifts his hand and waves weakly. "Papaw."

Sam crosses to the bed and gives a thumbs-up. "Scooter. It's good to have you back, buddy. You gave us a scare."

The boy rubs his oxygen mask, dislodging it. "Hurts," he murmurs.

"Hit a tree with that old sled, did you?"

Lisa readjusts Scooter's mask, then faces Sam. "Are you okay, Daddy?"

"I'm sorry, honey. All of a sudden it got to be too much for me. I don't know what happened. I kind of lost it." He hangs his head. "I should've stayed."

"Daddies get scared, too," I interject, praying Lisa will accept this explanation.

She starts to speak, then stops, as if pondering what I just said. "I guess I never thought about that. You always seem so in control, the strong one. You've been a hero to me. My own personal Super Dad."

"And now you've discovered I have feet of clay."

She smiles lovingly. "That's all right, just this one time."

"I was worried about Scooter and it reminded me of, well, of other times when…"

Lisa studies her father and, as if sensing the precariousness of his control, cuts him off. "It's okay, Daddy, honestly."

Sam holds out the spare chair, and I sink gratefully into it. After he leaves for a drugstore to buy first-aid cream for his hands, I close my eyes. The beep of the monitor and the hum of the window-unit heater are hypnotic. Just for a minute, I'll put my head back and drift.

"Yoohoo, I'm here."

I struggle to wake up. The first thing I see is Jenny and Lisa hugging each other. When they break apart, both are teary.

Jenny approaches the bed. "How's he doing? Don and I have been so worried."

She sits on the foot of the bed, rubbing Scooter's feet while Lisa fills her in. She is telling her sister about the possibility of the lung reinflating on its own, when Scooter stirs. "Where is he?"

"Who, honey?"

"My dad. I want my dad."

Lisa sends Jenny a despairing look, then adjusts her face into a calm smile. "He was here. Before you woke up. He promised to come back in the morning."

Scooter's fingers worry the edge of his blanket. "I thought…"

"He'll be here, just like he said."

After a while, Scooter drifts back to sleep. A nurse comes in and suggests that it's time for most of us to leave. Lisa gives us keys to her house and insists that we stay there.

To give Jenny and Lisa some time together, I wander to the waiting room. Five minutes later Sam steps off the elevator just as the girls appear. Lisa puts her arms around Sam and lays her head on his chest. "I love you, Daddy." She lowers her voice, but I can still hear her. "It's okay. Really. Everything is fine."

Then she moves to me. I give her a quick hug. "Call us if you need us. Remember, though, Scooter is in good hands."

A tall, athletic man with silver hair and intelligent gray eyes steps off the elevator and takes in the scene. He waits discreetly. "Lisa?" he finally says.

Our daughter takes one look at him and bursts into tears. "Hank. Oh, thank you for coming." He moves toward her and nestles her close. "Scooter's better, honey."

Jenny turns to me and mouths "Hank? *Him?*"

Sam has the look of a matador facing *el toro*.

I recover first. "I'm Isabel Lambert, Lisa's mother. She was hoping you'd be able to make it tonight."

He releases Lisa and holds out his hand. "I couldn't get here fast enough."

Sam glances from Hank to Lisa and I see the exact moment when he reaches a decision. "And I'm Lisa's father, Sam Lambert. It's good of you to come."

Lisa puts an arm around Jenny. "This is the sister from Colorado Springs I've told you so much about."

"I've looked forward to meeting you," Jenny says.

Then we all fall silent, depleted of social graces. A Down elevator stops and Sam moves to hold the door. "We were just leaving, Hank. C'mon, gals. We'll see you in the morning, Lisa."

Lisa waves. "Good night, everybody. I love you."

The elevator door is hardly shut before Jenny blurts, "Mother, this is more serious than I thought."

"I think maybe so."

"He's got some nerve showing up like one of the family." Sam growls.

I bow my head, on the verge of hysterical giggles.

Jenny folds her arms. "The way Lisa described him, I thought he was an old creep with gold chains looking for a young hottie. But he seemed, well, nice."

"Who knows? He may be just what she needs," I say. "Nothing is ever quite as it appears, is it, Sam?"

As if we are using a silent code, he nods. And takes my hand.

AFTER WE MAKE UP the beds, Jenny is wired and wants to talk. Sam, wrung out from his ordeal, goes to bed and, amazingly, I catch a second wind. Jenny settles me on the sofa and snugs an afghan around me. "Wine?" She doesn't wait for an answer, but heads to the kitchen.

The events of the past few hours swirl around me, but in the midst of it all, I recognize a blessing. Something about the crisis has brought out the best in all of us. I amend that judgment. Except for Neal. But that's hardly a surprise.

"Here." Jenny hands me a glass of red wine and curls up on the other end of the sofa. "What a scary time."

"Indeed. It was good of you to come."

"Lisa needs all the support she can get. I'll stick around for a few days, help her when Scooter gets out of the hospital."

"That would be great."

"I'm not being totally altruistic, Mom. I have an ulterior motive." She grins devilishly.

"Him?"

"Him. Hank may be quite a bit older, but I have to admit, he's gorgeous. Lisa kept going on and on about all the places he took her, so I assumed she was impressed with his money and lifestyle." She pauses to take a sip of wine. "But come to think of it, I never did ask her about his personality or character."

"Only time will tell. But she really seemed to need him at the hospital with her."

"I want her to be happy, Mom. It's a struggle being a single mom. While I'm here, I'll keep my eyes and ears open. By the end of my stay, I'll have the full Hank scoop."

I don't doubt it. Jenny is a bulldog when she has a mission. "Listen to Lisa with your heart, honey."

"I will." We sit in companionable silence for a while. Finally my exhaustion returns, and I yawn.

"What do you say we call it a night?" I suggest.

She folds the afghan over the back of the sofa and heads for Scooter's room. I turn off the lamp and tiptoe into the master bedroom. Sam is sprawled on his back, one arm flung on my side of the bed. In the light from the bathroom, I take off my clothes, put on my gown and brush my teeth. Slipping under the covers, I snuggle next to him, lulled by the rhythm of his breathing.

I wrap my arm around his solid chest and lie

awake staring into the darkness, my heart full of love for the brave, determined boy who weathered his father's abuse, the young man who dared to fly high above the earth, the heartbroken father who bore unexamined pain for years. And for the husband who, in his desiring the best for me, has guarded his own secrets.

Now, together, he and I have one last bridge to cross. Mark Taylor.

CHAPTER TWELVE

IN THE MORNING SAM and I stop by the hospital before leaving for home. Lisa is in the hallway, slumped against the wall. She straightens when she sees us. "Hi, Mom. Daddy."

Sam gives her a hug. "What're you doing out here?"

"Neal's with Scooter. I had to leave. He's promising him the sun and moon, as if he'll ever follow through."

"How was your night?" I ask by way of changing the subject.

"Long. I'd nod off, then jolt awake. I was so afraid Scooter would take a turn for the worse."

"And?"

"The nurses tell me he's better. The respiratory therapist and pulmonologist will be by later. We should know more then. But he feels pretty beat up."

"Broken ribs will do that. I don't imagine he'll be going sledding any time soon," Sam says with a sad smile. "But that's one heckuva bump on his head. His buddies will think he's really tough."

"I just want him home, safe and sound. This has been very scary. A kind of wake-up call."

We start walking toward the waiting room. "What do you mean?"

"I've been living as if everything is all about me. Resenting my heavy workload, letting bitterness about the divorce control me, feeling like a martyr as a single mom. Thinking other people should make me feel good about myself." She stops and faces Sam. "Even acting like Daddy was supposed to do everything for me, pamper me." She raises her hands in frustration. "Ye gods, I'm not a little girl. I have a son lying in there who could've died. But didn't. What's not to be thankful for? I'm getting the message loud and clear—it's grow-up-Lisa time."

Sam hugs her. "That all sounds well and good, but here's the thing. Even when you're old and gray you'll still be our little girl."

"I know that, Daddy. And I'm grateful to you and Mom. I love you guys so much."

We hang around until Neal, with a perfunctory nod in our direction, leaves and Jenny arrives.

The sisters stand, arms entwined, waiting with us at the elevator. Looking at them, my heart swells with love and pride, even as a voice inside asks what kind of man Blake would have become. This is a question without answers. One Sam and I will always live with.

Breckenridge, Colorado

ON THE DRIVE HOME, Sam holds my hand when traffic permits. We don't say much, respecting each other's unspoken need for reflection. One comfort of a long marriage is a connection that needs no words. Although the high elevations near Breckenridge are still frosted with snow, in the valleys most has melted or been cleared away. When we pick up the animals, Orville is aloof, but Sally threatens to lick us to death. Scratching her ears, I admit I'm glad Sam adopted her.

Once home, the familiar surroundings bring back the roller-coaster emotions of the past few days. We both know the time has come for us to deal with one more issue, and I suspect we are manufacturing chores in an effort to avoid the inevitable confrontation. Unpacking, making out a grocery list, putting in a load of wash, laying a fire, filling the bird feeders—whatever it takes.

Finally there's nothing left. Sam finds me in the kitchen unloading the dishwasher. Without speaking, he takes clean glasses out of the rack and puts them in the cupboard. When we finish,

I wipe down the counter. Then he says, "It's time, Izzy." He leads me into the family room and we sit in our chairs on either side of the fire. I know the outcome I'm hoping for, but in the same breath, I understand nothing is guaranteed.

Sam begins. "What happened to me last night shook me up. I was unprepared for the power of my emotions, especially after all this time. I realized something awful. We never talked about Blake, did we?"

I shake my head.

"Could we now, do you think?" The yearning in his voice touches a tender place deep within me.

"I think we must."

"Okay, then. I suspect you had no clue how desperately I wanted a son. Not just because that's the manly thing, but because I had something to prove. Every time my father took a swipe at me, cursed me, failed to show up for one of my games, I promised myself I would never be like that. My old man was a classic example of how not to parent. It sounds corny, but I would watch other guys' dads—how they clapped an arm around their sons after a ball game and bragged to folks in the café about their kids' grades. I wanted that so keenly, but I knew it was never going to happen. That all I could do was survive those years and move on. When I was thirteen, in the back of a notebook, I started a list of the things I would do if I ever had a son. Stuff like being a scoutmaster, hiking, buying him a car. You never knew this, but I kept that grimy list in my billfold until the day Blake died and I tore it into a hundred pieces."

I watch Sam struggle with his memories.

"When he was born, I thought I had the world by the tail. I had this beautiful wife who loved me, an adorable daughter, and now the perfect son. I know what the experts say. That babies don't recognize people at first, but I don't believe it. He would stare at me, as if he were memorizing my face. Then he'd grab my finger with this really firm grasp. Remember how I used to say he'd be holding a bat in no time?"

"And the jeans? You came home from the store one day with these tiny denim overalls and insisted I dress him in them even though they were three inches too long."

Sam smiles tenderly. "I'd forgotten that. But I sure didn't want him in any sissy clothes."

"He wasn't going to be a sissy, not with the way you were tossing him in the air, teaching him how to 'fly' at five months."

"I loved it when I'd watch a televised game with Jenny cuddled on one side and Blake on the other. I swear he'd study the TV as if he understood everything the commentators were saying."

He stretched out his legs and sighed. "Oh, Izzy, I had such dreams for him."

"So did I."

He sat up and leaned forward. "What were yours?"

My eyes grow misty. "Oh, the usual. That he would succeed in school and value learning, fulfill his potential whether that was following in your footsteps or not, find a mate worthy of him."

"We had him such a short time."

"Yet he had a powerful effect." Then an idea occurs to me. "Remember the box I wrote you about. The one where I kept some of his things. Would you like to see it?"

"I'm not sure I can do it."

"These memories are painful, but if we're to heal…"

"All right then, go get it."

I locate it easily. No matter where we've moved, I've always known where it is. I move the blanket on my closet shelf and retrieve the antique wooden box. Rubbing my hand over the walnut lid with an inlaid sailboat in the center, I cradle the memory of Blake to myself for just a moment before I return to the family room.

Kneeling beside Sam, I lay the box in his lap. He sits lost in his thoughts before tentatively raising the lid. First he looks at the baptismal certificate, then at the birth certificate. He traces a finger across the inky imprint of a tiny foot. "He was so little." Finally he puts the documents on the coffee table and with a strangled laugh lifts out the tiny blue baseball cap with NY entwined on the front. "Do you think he'd have been a Yankee fan, too?"

I understand it's a rhetorical question. Sam turns the cap in his hands, remembering. Reaching in the box, I pull out a white flannel blanket with blue lambs, leaving the white leather baby shoes in the bottom. I bring the blanket to my face, desperate to inhale once more that special new-baby smell.

Sam picks up one end and rubs it between his fingers. "Remember how Jenny would find the blanket and throw it in his crib and say, 'Baby, need a bankie'?"

I lay my head on his knee. This is pain, but not the stabbing kind. It is the ache of nostalgia.

"We didn't forget him, did we, Izzy?"

"Never."

"Why haven't we talked like this before? Or looked at the box or photographs?"

"I thought you wouldn't want to." I gaze into his eyes. "But there's another reason."

"What's that?"

"All these years I thought you blamed me."

"Blamed you? For what?"

"Blake's death."

"Are you out of your mind? How can you even say that?"

"Because we won't be finished until we remember that day."

He sets the box on the floor, then takes the blanket from me, tossing it aside. He pulls me up and curls me into his lap, running his fingers through my hair. "Oh, Izzy, I'm so sorry."

Heart thudding, I begin. "You came home. I was sitting in the rocker, holding Blake. I just rocked and rocked. Other people were there, but I can't tell you who. I only knew I needed to hold on to my baby. Then you came in and—"

"Went berserk," Sam says quietly.

"Yes. You lashed out at everybody, then put your fist through the wall. Someone took Blake from me, but by then you were gone. And I knew. It was my fault. I was the one at home. I was the one in the kitchen drinking coffee, instead of checking on my son. You were right to blame me!"

"Izzy, honestly, the only person I blamed was myself. What kind of a man can't even protect his own family?"

"In our own ways, each of us was searching for a scapegoat. It was inconceivable that a perfectly healthy baby could die, just like that. Nobody knew much about SIDS back then. The doctors could talk until they were blue in the face, but I didn't believe our son's death was the result of a mysterious cause. The explanation was simple. I had failed Blake."

"And I didn't tell you any different. Jeesh! What a thoughtless, selfish jerk I was. You must've felt as if you'd lost both your son and your husband."

"You couldn't talk about it, Sam. Not to the chaplain, not to your buddies." I strangle on my tears. "And most of all not to me. So I couldn't talk, either."

He pulls me even closer. "One night, not too long after Blake died, you came to bed after I did. I pretended to be asleep. And you tried, Izzy, you really did. You put your arms around me and snuggled so close. I knew you wanted me, wanted a connection. I shut my eyes and clenched my teeth. It took every ounce of willpower to keep from turning to you."

"Why?"

"Because I knew I'd come apart like I did last night. The only way I could function was to bury my emotions right along with my son. But…" his voice is anguished "…I forgot about the most important thing in my life. You."

"We both went a bit crazy."

"Still, that doesn't make it right."

"Did you…did you ever visit Blake's grave when we were stationed in Tampa again?"

He can't look at me. "No. Too painful." We sit in silence until he manages the question I know he's been waiting to ask. "Did you?"

"Often." I picture the serenity of that lush green cemetery and the finality of a child-size headstone. "Would you like to go there together sometime?"

His voice chokes. "Yes. Yes, I would."

I reach out and caress his cheek. "Nothing will ever change what happened. The only thing that makes sense is to honor our son's memory by remembering his short little life with all the joy we can muster."

"I'm sorry, Izzy."

"I'm sorry, too. But yesterday is gone."

He smooths back my hair and kisses my forehead. "But never, ever forgotten."

BEFORE WE CAN CONTINUE the conversation, we are interrupted by a neighbor who needs Sam's help to move some furniture. He seems relieved, as if he's been given a reprieve from where our conversation has to go next. The past was about the son he lost. The future requires a decision about the son he has. If he's ever to have true peace…

I get up and move to the bookshelves. The

billiken stares down at me, his omniscient smile a dare. I pick him up, caressing his smooth body, then turn him over and, with my fingers, trace the letters on the bottom. *The god of things as they ought to be.*

I take one last look at the billiken before replacing him on the shelf. I've made my decision. Sometimes you can't rely on the gods. You have to take matters into your own hands.

Before I can reconsider, I go to the phone, dial the number and wait, nerves on edge. When he answers, I say simply, "Mark, it's time for you to come."

THE FURNITURE-MOVING PROJECT turned out to be more than Sam had bargained for. The upside was that he needed to blow off the steam generated by the last couple of days.

Sally welcomed him back into the house and followed him into the kitchen where Izzy was baking. "What got into you?" he asked, snitching a glob of cookie dough. She made a play of slapping his hand.

"I'm keeping my mind occupied until we hear more about Scooter."

"Lisa will call when she knows anything new." He nuzzled the back of her neck. "Just think of it. I have a sexy wife who can cook, too. I'm a lucky man."

She turned, smiling girlishly. "And they said it would never last."

"That was certainly your mother's opinion."

"But you made inroads when you brought her that silk kimono from Bangkok."

"She was something else, all right. No secret where you get the take-charge gene." He grinned at her and went upstairs to shower and change.

He dressed in cords and a plaid flannel shirt. Izzy was still fussing in the kitchen, so after retrieving the metal lock box from the garage, he went to his office. Once at the desk, he sat staring at the box. In Montana, he'd read some of Izzy's letters, but deliberately hadn't looked at them all. He couldn't. Now he needed to. Thumbing through the stack, he located one dated shortly after their reunion in Hawaii.

Sam, it's only been two weeks and yet it seems an eternity since we were sunning on Waikiki Beach. The days passed in a blur, didn't they? I think it was hard for us to be totally natural with each other. At least it was for me. I have no comprehension, really, of what you're going through, so I didn't want to say or do the wrong thing while we were together. I know these long separations are part of the bargain, but they can sure put a

strain on a marriage. I'm hoping in our letters we can be honest with one another, so
that when you come home, we'll have a
headstart on our post-war relationship.

He remembered distinctly when he'd received
this letter. It had arrived about a month after he'd
written Diane the "Dear Jane" letter. Even then
he'd had second thoughts. The transition from
Hawaii back into the hostilities was a jolt. Living
on the edge of danger, being available practically
around the clock, the impermanence of anything—all took its toll. That's when he began
thinking again about Diane. Intellectually he'd
understood calling things off with her was the
right thing, but he'd been so damn lonely.

It had been a moot point, anyway. He'd known
Diane's tour ended six weeks after he came back
from Honolulu and that she would be returning to
the States.

His coping device was to daydream about Izzy
and Jenny, picturing their little family living an
idealized version of the American dream. House
in the suburbs, white picket fence and all. The
three of them would be a unit. His wife and
daughter the perfect complement to the ambitious
young officer rising through the ranks.

Sam shook his head. The naiveté of it all. Then

had come the letter that changed everything. It was near the bottom of the stack.

Sam, I have some news, and I hope you'll be as thrilled about this as I am. I'm pregnant. Call me silly, but I'm convinced it happened that last night in Hawaii. I felt at the time as if you were pouring your whole being into me. And now we will have living proof of that. When you come home, we'll have not only a new life, but a new baby.

He held the letter between trembling fingers, the emotions of that long-ago time surfacing against his will. He'd been sitting on his cot in the officers' quarters. Ripping open the envelope, he'd scanned Izzy's familiar handwriting until coming to the words *I'm pregnant*. Something like an electric charge had passed through him. *Blake*. The cry in his chest mounted on a crest of hysteria. He'd bolted from the barracks and walked as fast as he could, ignoring the non-coms who saluted, intent on nothing but putting distance between himself and the letter.

Now, when he reflected on that former self, he bit his lip in disgust. But at the time, his immediate and irrational thought had been that Izzy had deliberately planned the pregnancy.

He recalled thinking she was trying to replace their son. He'd been furious. God help him, he hadn't wanted this new baby—it was too threatening. And what if it was a boy?

Sam reread the letter and realized, perhaps for the first time, what the pregnancy must've meant to Izzy. An end to the total darkness of grief and separation, a new beginning, hope.

Setting the letter aside, he bowed his head, faced with his callow insensitivity. He couldn't remember how he'd answered Izzy. Probably with platitudes like "Take care of yourself" or "It'll be nice for Jenny to have a playmate." Bottom line, he'd experienced none of the joy he had with the other two pregnancies.

Then, like a blinding shaft of light, a thought struck him. Lisa. Oh, God. Had he welcomed a second daughter as a loving father? Or had he held her at arm's length, punishing her for not being Blake?

The demands of the years echoed in his consciousness. "I wuv you, Daddy, but you never come out to play wif me." "Daddy, please, please put that paper down and read to me." "I mean it, Daddy, I need you to fix my bike *now*." He tilted back in the desk chair, arms dangling loosely at his side, the guilt of forty years making an old man of him. "Daddy, come fix the dishwasher."

What kind of a sorry excuse of a father had he been? Something had always prevented him from giving Lisa the full attention she deserved. The reason was patently obvious. He'd been afraid to get too close. On some level, she'd been begging for only one thing: unconditional love from her father. *God help her. God help him.*

THE PHONE STARTLED HIM out of his funk and he grabbed up the receiver. "Dad?"

He heard a click and Izzy chimed in. "Jenny, I'm here, too."

"I have guarded good news. The doctors will keep Scooter in the hospital a couple of more days as a precaution. He's had trouble remembering a few things, but they're confident that will clear up. His lung seems to be inflating on its own, but they're going to continue monitoring his progress."

There was a lilt in Izzy's voice. "That sounds very positive. How's Lisa?"

"She's walking Hank out to the car. She'll be back in a minute. You might be interested to know the man in question has been here all day." She paused, and he suspected she was whetting her mother's curiosity.

"Jenny, you're holding out on us," Izzy said.

"Just having a little fun. Mom, I have to tell you, I think Hank's okay. Even more than okay. He's been very attentive to Lisa, and I feel quite comfortable around him. He's really very kind and thoughtful."

"What's Scooter's reaction to him?"

"He wasn't thrilled at first. In fact, he turned away and wouldn't look at him, but Hank was patient and didn't force the issue. When Lisa went to get us coffee this afternoon, Hank started talking about football and Scooter couldn't help thawing, especially when Hank mentioned that one of the Denver Broncos lives in the same condominium unit as he does. Hank promised to bring Scooter an autographed football. That did it. They've made a start."

Sam inquired about the memory loss. "It's apparently quite normal for patients to forget the event that caused the concussion. Scooter has no recollection of hitting the tree. And he didn't remember being taken to X-ray."

"Are you staying on?" Izzy asked.

"Yes. I'm at loose ends with the girls in school and Don in Albuquerque on business, so I'll be here to help." There was silence on the line and then Jenny said, "Here comes Lisa. Do you want to say hello?"

Sam spoke first. "Lisa? We're happy things are going well. And we're looking forward to spending time with Hank." What the hell. He could be generous if the guy was good to his daughter and grandson. "But that's not the main thing I want to say."

"I'm listening, Daddy."

From the depths of his being, he simply said, "I love you, honey."

IZZY HAD FIXED A pot roast with potatoes, carrots, onions and her signature brown gravy. She set a bowl of asparagus on the table and took her seat beside him. Nodding at him, she said, "I think a blessing is in order."

His mind flooded with impressions. He paused to collect himself. "Gracious God, Izzy and I thank you for holding Scooter in your hands and for reminding us of what is precious." He hesitated, reflecting on words that came from knowledge gained over the past few days. "For the gifts of family, honesty and love. Bless us all and bless the food we are about to eat. Amen."

"Thank you," Izzy said quietly, passing him the platter of roast and browned vegetables. "Do you remember when Jenny broke her arm? How worried we were?"

He was immediately transported to a Tucson emergency room. While performing a cheerleading stunt, she'd fallen. His clerk had located him on the base and he'd raced to the hospital, panicky for information. "It could've been a lot worse. We were lucky."

"I imagine that's how Lisa's feeling about now. No matter how hard we try, we can't always protect our children."

Sam knew she was thinking of Blake, as was he. "Most of them are pretty resilient."

She spooned gravy over her meat and potatoes and handed him the gravy boat. "You obviously were."

He'd never thought of himself as resilient. "I survived, that's all."

"What would you say to your father if you could?"

"Are you trying to ruin a fella's dinner?"

Setting down her fork, she raised an eyebrow, and he understood she deserved the truth.

He picked up a roll and buttered it carefully. "First, I'd ask all kinds of questions. Did you love my mother? Did you and my mother want children? Did I imagine it, or were you a pretty good guy before Mom died? Why did you start drinking? Did you resent Lloyd and me that much? Did you even know that you were hurting us?" He hesitated, then blurted out the hardest one of all. "Did you ever love us?"

"Would knowing the answers help you?"

He considered her question. "Answers wouldn't

change who I am, but they might make me more able to forgive him." He took a swig of water. "What brought this up? Our conversation about Blake?"

She smiled fondly. "I can't tell you what a relief it is to be able to talk about Blake, to hear you drop his name into a conversation like that."

"Maybe remembering him will help. He was a part of our family, after all." As he uttered the words, he wondered why it had taken him so long to arrive at this point.

"Yes, he was." Her smile faded.

"You haven't eaten much," he observed.

She glanced at Sally standing in the kitchen door. "Silly dog. She's hoping for my leftovers."

"Aren't you hungry?"

She didn't answer the question. Instead she said, "You asked why I brought up your father. I think it bothers you that you never really knew him. The *real* him, the man your mother fell in love with."

The hackles on his neck rose. "Where are you going with this?"

"Remember how you used to tease me about being the commander of the Lambert family?"

"Who was teasing?" He hoped his joking banter would distract her. It didn't.

"I've made a decision. Not only that, I've acted on it."

He didn't like the sound of this. "What're you talking about?"

"You've lost a son. You had a father whom you never really knew. Mark Taylor is your son. He doesn't know his father. But he wants to. He needs to."

Like a razor, his voice cut through the silence. "What have you done, Isabel?"

"We need to lay the ghosts to rest and embrace every single member of this family. I've invited Mark to come back here to meet you."

He shoved his chair back so hard, it clattered to the floor. "You had no right."

Izzy stood, too. "I had every right, Sam Lambert. You can't put this off the way you put off mourning Blake." She gestured at Sally. "Look there. You brought home a dirty, stray dog and welcomed her into your heart. Can't you do as much for your own flesh and blood?"

He thought of Blake, lying cold in Izzy's arms. Of Lisa, from whom he'd withheld affection and approval. Of a loving, vulnerable and young—oh, so young—woman with silver-blond hair and gentle gray eyes who glued him back together in a jigsaw world gone mad. This wasn't easy, but Izzy knew him better than he knew himself. And still she loved him. He shrugged in capitulation. "When?"

"Day after tomorrow."

FOLLOWING BREAKFAST THE next morning, unable to settle down to any task, Sam took Sally for a walk. Staying close beside him, Sally only occasionally darted off after a chipmunk or bird. It was a spectacular Colorado day. On the mountains, evergreens gave way to masses of aspen-gold. The brisk, pine-scented air was the tonic he needed.

His instinct to walk at a breakneck pace was an indication of his need to escape. The more he tried to anticipate what he'd say or do tomorrow, what Mark would say or do, the more he tensed up. His immediate reaction last night had been to lash out at Izzy for her presumption, her interference. But, as usual, his wife was right. His pattern of fleeing from emotional challenges had to be broken. Too many had been hurt by his actions. Izzy, most of all, but Lisa and Jenny, as well. Diane. And her son. *His* son.

Stunned, he stopped dead. He'd actually done it—owned the words. *My son.*

At Sally's insistence, they started slowly toward the tarn. For so long, with each of Blake's birthdays, he would drive himself nuts computing how old his boy would've been had he lived, what he would've looked like, what interests he'd have pursued, what sports he might have enjoyed. In the process, Sam had invented a life for his son, one in which he'd played a central role as father.

He had no such frame of reference for Mark Taylor. So long as he preserved him as a paper cutout of a man, he could pretend Mark didn't exist and hadn't anything to do with him. But the truth? He'd heard Mark's voice on the answering machine. His son was real.

Deep in thought, he became aware of his surroundings again only when they reached the water's edge. "Time to turn around, girl. Make our way back."

As they walked along, he was struck by what he'd just said. Was that what he was doing? Making his way back? Back to a time when he'd harbored no secrets? To a time when he might have earned the adoration in Izzy's beautiful brown eyes?

A couple of weeks ago, when she'd called him a coward, she'd scored a bull's-eye. He was tired of running from himself. Tomorrow, once and for all, he had to bury one son and open his heart to another.

NOW THAT THE DAY of Mark Taylor's visit had dawned, oddly it was Izzy who was nervous, and Sam who was calm. She kept glancing at him out of the corner of her eye, as if trying to gauge his mood. "Should I plan on him for dinner?"

"We'll have to play that by ear."

"I think you'll like him, Sam."

"Izzy, listen to yourself. If you could wind me up and program me, you would. You can't expect instant bonding."

"I know, I know. I suppose lots of wives would be resentful of someone intruding into their family. But, Sam, I feel so good about this. It's the right thing to do."

"It's a mistake to have expectations. This meeting will unfold as it will."

"Do you want me there?"

"Yes, at least, at first. Later? We'll just have to see."

Lisa called just before noon to tell them that Scooter would be dismissed the next day. During their conversation, Sam asked if he could come see her later in the week. "Oh, Daddy," she said. "Hank already fixed the dishwasher for me." For a split second Sam admitted he wasn't sure he wanted to be replaced as her go-to guy, but then he recovered. "Glad to hear it, but that's not why I'm coming. I want to spend some time with you. Talk about some things." The surprise and pleasure in her voice was flattering. However, what he had to tell her might affect the welcome he received.

After lunch, he and Sally took another walk,

and he acknowledged the source of his peace of mind. It was the same sensation he'd experienced sitting in the cockpit revving the engines for another bombing run over enemy territory. Nothing at that point could be changed. Events now, as then, were out of his control. What would be, would be.

CHAPTER THIRTEEN

Breckenridge, Colorado

A LITTLE BEFORE THREE, Sam changed out of his jeans into gray flannel slacks, a red turtleneck and his favorite blue pullover. Izzy had gone into her closet three times, deliberating her wardrobe choice. Finally she came out wearing deep purple slacks and a lavender silk blouse with matching cashmere cardigan. Around her neck were the pearls and matching earrings he'd given her after Blake's birth.

Taking her in his arms, he held her close for several moments. Her signature floral perfume filled his senses. He kissed her temple before whispering, "No matter what, Isabel Lambert, you are the best wife any man could have. Thank you for helping me reach this day."

"It's an opportunity, Sam."

"I hope so." He released her. "I'm ready."

As if on cue, the doorbell rang.

On their way through the family room, Izzy paused, removed the billiken from the bookshelf and cradled the figure in her hands briefly before placing him on the coffee table. Then she went to the door as they'd decided in advance she would do.

Sam waited by the fireplace, his only company, the billiken. Suddenly his entire body relaxed. The know-it-all grin on the little guy's face was a good omen. *Things as they ought to be.* However that turned out.

"Please come on in," he heard Izzy say.

A deep baritone voice answered. "I can't tell you what this means to me, Mrs. Lambert."

And then Mark Taylor stood before him. He didn't know what he'd expected, but a dozen sensations washed over him. The young man was tall, dressed just as Sam was in gray flannel slacks, a turtleneck and a pullover sweater, although his was forest green. Eyes the color of Sam's widened in recognition. When Sam extended his hand, he noticed Mark was almost exactly his same height. His short blond hair was cut just as his was when he'd had more hair. "I'm Mark," he said, searching Sam's face for a reaction. "Thank you for agreeing to meet me."

Sam's heart pounded. "My…my wife deserves the credit." Looking at him was like looking in the mirror—the long nose, close-set ears and square jaw. Yet in the silver cast to Mark's hair and the depths of his tranquil expression, Sam found Diane, and the resemblance stopped his breath.

He didn't know how long they stood there, each studying the other, until Izzy suggested they sit down. Mark sat on one end of the sofa, Izzy on the other. Sam sought refuge in his leather recliner. Awkwardness hung over them like a thick cloud. He cleared his throat. "I see Diane in you."

"I take that as a compliment. My mother was a beautiful person, inside and out." He turned to Izzy. "Mrs. Lambert, I hope this isn't too painful for you." Then he looked at Sam. "Or for you. I debated long and hard before I made the decision to search for you. I know this isn't easy having me come and upset you and your family."

Sam surprised himself by saying, "But it had to happen."

Mark nodded in agreement. "I'm relieved you feel that way. Since I was little, I've had this feeling that something wasn't quite right. That I didn't totally belong. I used to fantasize that I'd been dropped into the Taylor family from an alien spaceship. I can't tell you where I got such a notion, but it's been with me as long as I can remember. Somewhere, someplace, I kept thinking, is the answer."

Sam struggled to understand. "Didn't you grow up thinking Diane's husband was your father?"

"Yes, that's the way she wanted it. When she left Southeast Asia, she came back to Georgia and eloped with her high school sweetheart, Rolf Taylor. His is the name on my birth certificate. He's the man I call Dad."

"Did he know you weren't his biological son?"

"Yes, but I didn't find out myself until after my mother died eighteen months ago."

"Why did she keep it a secret?"

Mark gestured at Izzy and around the room, then turned to Sam. "This. All of this. Rolf told me she never wanted to disrupt your family. She understood you were happily married. She went into her relationship with you with her eyes wide open, or so she thought." He bowed his head. "I don't think she expected to be hurt."

Sam shifted uneasily in his chair. "What makes you say that?"

"Dad told me she loved you very much."

Izzy uttered a sharp mewl of sympathy.

"Did she tell him that?"

He smiled sadly. "No, he said he just knew. But I don't want to leave the wrong impression. She loved Rolf, too."

Izzy spoke for the first time. "Your dad must care a great deal about you to give you the information you needed to find Sam."

"He does. And I love him. Without our close relationship, I could never have told him how important this is to me."

Sam couldn't help it. He found himself admiring the man's honesty and sense of purpose. "How can I help?"

"I have questions, Col. Lambert."

"Please, call me Sam."

"And me, Izzy." Rising to her feet, Izzy asked if they would like coffee or a soft drink.

"Black coffee would be great," Mark said.

Another thing he and Sam had in common. "Likewise."

After she left, Mark apologized again. "I didn't want to inflict this on your wife."

"Actually, she took it better than I did. I've had some issues getting to this point. But she's helped me. My wife is an amazing woman."

"I can tell."

When Izzy returned and handed Sam a mug of coffee, he took a sip, then turned to Mark. "Fire away with the questions."

"How did you meet my mother?"

In Mark's Southern drawl, Sam heard the melodic cadence of Diane's voice. He cleared his throat and told the story just as he'd told it to Izzy, and as he did, once again that faraway place came alive in memory. When he'd finished, he looked at his wife, begging her understanding as he added, "I imagine you want to know about my feelings for your mother."

Mark glanced at Izzy with concern. "If you'd like to tell me."

Sam cupped his hands around the mug, drawing warmth and will into his body. "She was my port in the storm. That's the clearest way I can put it. Simply put, flying in combat was terrifying, the adrenaline rushes, unrelenting. Home seemed millions of miles and eons away. Izzy wasn't there. I craved a sanctuary. Your mother provided it. I would never intentionally have hurt her." Suddenly weary, he set down the mug and waited.

"Thank you for that. I would hate to think I owed my existence to a one-night stand."

"Quite the contrary. I cherished her."

In the momentary silence, Orville padded across the floor, jumped into Mark's lap and settled there, his purrs audible. "Nice cat," Mark remarked, running his hand down Orville's back.

Izzy smiled at the picture the two of them made. "Orville is a very good judge of character."

It was true. This was a fine young man sitting on their sofa. Sam tried yet again to wrap his mind around the fact that the man was his son.

"Sir, you mentioned you've had issues surrounding my appearance in your lives. Can we talk about them?"

Izzy and Sam exchanged glances. He was reluctant to bare his soul again. Sharing with a virtual stranger what he'd only recently admitted to his wife was hard. But Mark's honesty deserved no less in return. "The most obvious difficulty was learning about your existence, because I never dreamed Diane was pregnant. Naturally, too, I've been concerned about the impact not only on Izzy, but my family."

"You have children?"

Damn, it hadn't occurred to him that Mark didn't know. "Yes, two daughters. Jenny who's older than you, and Lisa who's about your age." His voice was hoarse as he ventured into topics that were still raw. "And we had a son. Blake. That's the big issue for me."

"If you'd rather not, sir—"

"Please. It's Sam." He took a deep breath and began. "Shortly before I left for Southeast Asia, we lost our five-month-old son. Sudden Infant Death Syndrome." Izzy's expression was heartrending. He kept forgetting that she couldn't always be the strong one, that she, too, still grieved Blake.

"I'm very sorry."

"He was the answer to my prayer. My own father was negligent and abusive. Blake was the light of my life, the means by which I could prove that I was nothing like my dad. God, I had such high hopes for him."

During the interval while he tried to get a grip, Orville hopped down and came over to him. He rubbed against Sam's leg before scampering from the room. "I couldn't accept his death. My way of dealing with it was to shut out everyone I cared about. We were trained in the military to be in control, to command the situation. I hid my grief behind that facade and carried it into battle. Until I could carry it no longer. That's where your mother came into the picture. She was the safe place where I could begin to talk about Blake. But even then, I didn't let down my guard very far. Diane's understanding took just enough pressure off to enable me to function."

Izzy came around behind his chair, put her arms around him and kissed the top of his head. "I know this is difficult, Sam. But you're doing fine. I'm okay with it. So, please, tell Mark the rest. It has a lot to do with where the two of you go from here." She kissed him again and returned to the sofa.

Without that show of support, he couldn't have gone on. About Izzy's pregnancy and his feelings concerning another baby. About his deep-seated fear the child would be a boy. And then the really hard part. "I can't describe to you the guilt I felt. And shame. I was supposed to be this competent, fearless warrior yet I'd been helpless to save my own son. The solutions? I flew off to war and had an affair. I didn't plan it, I wasn't proud of it, but that guilt had nothing whatsoever to do with Diane. She was pure light. It had to do with my own weakness. And my battered, misguided ego."

Sam could no longer sit still. He stood, rubbing his hands together. "Now, here's the worst. When Izzy told me you had come here, I wanted absolutely nothing to do with you. I didn't want to acknowledge my relationship with your mother. I didn't want anything to rock my family's boat or to jeopardize their opinion of me. In short, I didn't want you." He shrugged helplessly. "So there you have it."

Mark scrubbed his hands across his face in a gesture that Sam recognized as his own. "Give me a minute."

Izzy rose to her feet, picked up our empty mugs and disappeared into the kitchen. Sam knew she was deliberately leaving them alone. He also knew that how he responded in the next five minutes was critical.

"Sam," Mark began, "I didn't come here expecting to be welcomed as a son. I'm grateful for anything you can tell me and for your honesty, but if you think I'm judging you, rest assured, I'm not. We're way beyond that. Even with your descriptions, I can't begin to imagine what it's like to lose a child or to fight a war. But I do know about feeling lost. Thanks to you and your wife, I have the missing piece to the puzzle that is me. I am eternally grateful."

Unmanly tears threatened. To stem them Sam said, "Mark, are you a drinking man? I think it's time to break out the Glenlivet."

"I'd be much obliged, Sam."

They both stood and started to shake hands, but then impulsively, Sam held out his arms, and as he embraced his son, he no longer cared about shutting off the waterworks.

Izzy chose that moment to enter the room. "Well, I declare." She beamed at the two of them. As he and Mark broke apart, Izzy first hugged Mark and then Sam. And with that smug expression he knew so well, she marched to the coffee table, picked up the billiken, shot Sam a triumphant smile and returned the little god to his perch on the shelf.

Over drinks they shared stories—Sam's career, their growing up, Mark's law practice. In the process it was eerie how many interests they had in common. The longer they talked, the more convinced Sam became of something new and important. He liked this man.

When Mark pulled out his billfold to show them photographs of his wife Sue and his family, Sam studied the picture of six-year-old twin boys, dressed in Little League soccer uniforms, grinning toothless grins. With a hitch in his voice, Mark introduced Sam to his grandsons.

WITH EACH PASSING MOMENT, each conversation, Sam became increasingly comfortable. Over dinner, Mark clarified that he had no intention of horning in on their family and, in the same breath, assured them that the nature of any future relationship would be up to them. On the one hand, Sam was relieved, but on the other, he found himself wanting to reach out to Mark and his family. Strangely, despite his forty-year ignorance of Mark's existence, he felt deeply connected to him.

As Mark prepared to leave, he told them an upcoming trial compelled him to return to Georgia, but he handed them his card, saying, "If you decide you're comfortable doing so, I'd really like to hear from you again." Sam saw in Mark's eyes the same yearning Izzy had described after his initial visit.

Sam laid his hands on Mark's shoulders. "You will, son. You will. Please, just give us time to prepare our family."

Izzy stepped forward and kissed Mark on the cheek. "Thank you for coming on such short notice."

"Nothing was more important, although I have

to tell you, after that first visit, it was hard to wait." His smile encompassed them both. "But it was worth it."

Then he looked at Sam tentatively, as if unsure of the protocol. "Hell, Mark, let's not stand on ceremony." And they embraced again, fumblingly, satisfyingly.

After clearing the table and loading the dishwasher, Izzy and Sam returned to the family room to replay the evening. Orville, perched alertly in Izzy's lap, seemed an interested though neutral observer. Izzy was the first to speak. She applauded Sam's efforts. "I knew you and Mark would get along. Oh, honey, I see so much of you in him."

Though relieved that Izzy liked Mark, he still didn't feel totally comfortable with the situation. Beyond worrying about Jenny's and Lisa's reactions, he had to be certain Izzy wasn't talking herself into something she would ultimately regret.

"…and isn't his wife a gem? And the way he talks about her, why, anyone can tell—"

He stopped her in midsentence. "Izzy, I need to ask you something."

Her jaw dropped. "You're so serious. Is something wrong? Have I misread the signals?"

"You misread nothing. But you have to be completely honest. Can you truly accept Mark? After all, he will be a constant reminder of Diane, of my infidelity."

Pulling an afghan around her shoulders, she didn't immediately answer. "What you're really asking is whether I forgive you."

"I suppose so." He studied his hands, unwilling to face her, fearful of her answer.

"I was mad as hell when I first found out. I felt stupid, demeaned, humiliated. Like what kind of rock had I been living under during those years? When you traipsed off to Montana, refusing to face the situation, I felt abandoned, as if you'd betrayed me again. In retrospect, though, maybe that separation was good. It gave me time to think about a lot of things. Especially Blake. And after a while, I began trying to walk in your moccasins.

"You need to know one thing, Sam. Never in these past days have I ever stopped loving you, not for a minute."

Biting his lip, he stared at the ceiling. He didn't deserve this woman. Never had.

"Do I forgive you?" She moved Orville, crossed the room and knelt at his feet. "It was all a long time ago and given the horror of Blake's death and the stress of that craziness in Vietnam…" Her voice faded as she looked into her husband's eyes. "Of course, I forgive you." She laid her head on his knee. "There's a more important issue. Can you forgive yourself?"

He considered her question. "Maybe, in time. But I'm worried about the girls. How do we tell them?"

"Don't sell them short, Sam."

"I think I'd like to get to know Mark. I want to meet his family."

"Of course you do. Jenny and Lisa will understand."

"If they do, it's only because of the wonderful mother they have."

"And the fact that they love their father enough to want his happiness."

Happiness. He hadn't experienced that state in years. "Izzie, from the time Blake died, I thought I could never be happy again. Now I'm not so sure." He paused, recalling the handsome, sensitive young man he'd met this evening. "Mark Taylor is not Blake. But, Izzie, you were right. He is my son."

SEVERAL DAYS AFTER Mark's visit, Izzy and Sam stopped on their way to Boulder at a mall to pick up some books and puzzles for Scooter. He was home and doing well, but still needed to be kept quiet. The plan was for Izzy to entertain Scooter while Sam told Lisa his story. Despite having carefully rehearsed what he would say, he couldn't help being apprehensive. Then from Boulder, they planned to drive on to Colorado Springs to tell Jenny and Don about Mark.

When they arrived shortly after noon, Lisa greeted them and ushered them into the living room. Scooter was sprawled under a blanket on the sofa, his fingers playing over the keyboard of an electronic game. When he saw his grandparents, he broke into a grin. "Mamaw, Papaw, yea! You're here."

"Hey, buddy," Sam said. "You're a whole lot better than the last time we saw you."

As if fearful of losing out on a bid for sympathy, the boy said, "But I still hurt."

Izzy leaned over to kiss his forehead. "I'll bet you do." She set down the shopping bag, settled on the sofa, picked up Scooter's feet and laid them in her lap.

"Did you bring me anything?"

Lisa shook her head. "You little rascal, I told you not to ask."

"I forgot," he said sheepishly. "But did you?"

Izzy reached in the bag and handed him a Spider-Man jigsaw puzzle.

"Cool. Me and Hank have been having fun working puzzles. He likes Spider-Man, you know."

"Why don't you tell me about your friend Hank?"

Lisa rolled her eyes. "Mom!"

Sam smothered a grin. Izzy was incorrigible. In short order, she would mine more information than he could in a week.

Lisa excused herself to put some laundry in the dryer. Too nervous to sit, Sam wandered into the kitchen. Lisa found him there. "What're you looking for, Daddy?"

"I thought I'd make a pot of coffee."

Her face fell. "I'm sorry, but I haven't had a chance to run to the store."

He seized the opportunity. "Here's an idea. Why don't you and I have a Starbucks date and afterward we can stop by the supermarket. Your mother will take good care of Scooter. We won't be gone long." In his nervousness, he was rambling.

"I hate to leave Scooter." Then, shrugging, she said, "But you're right. Mom's had more experience mothering than I have. Besides, you said you had something to talk with me about. Okay, let's go."

On the way for coffee, Lisa surprised him. "Like Mom, you're probably wondering about Hank."

He said nothing. When Lisa was ready to talk, the best plan was to listen.

"I know he's quite a bit older, but I like that. He's mature, something I could never say about Neal. At first, I thought we were just having fun and never dreamed the relationship was going anywhere. Hank never pressured me, but the more time I spent with him, the more I missed him when we were apart. And, oh, Daddy, the way he's been with Scooter these past few days? How can I not love someone who takes such good care of both of us?"

Sam wasn't ready for the *love* word, but when he looked at his daughter, she was radiant. All the tension that had lined her face for months was gone. "If you're happy, that's all that matters."

How happy would she be, though, when he told her his news?

Starbucks wasn't busy, so they picked up their cappuccinos and headed for a window table. "This is nice," she said. "I haven't been out and about in a while."

"Are you having to use up vacation days from work?"

"Yes, but Scooter's worth it."

He reached across the table to wipe a dollop of whipped cream off her nose.

She giggled. "Feels like old times."

Sam gripped his cup and plunged in. "It's those old times I want to talk about."

"Sounds mysterious."

"Let me start by telling you about your brother Blake." It never got any easier to talk about his son's death.

"As a mother, I can only imagine what torment

you and Mom went through. This scare with Scooter terrified me."

"I appreciate your understanding, but there's more to it." He stared into his cup, then raised his head and looked directly at his daughter. "Because I've only recently been able to deal with my grief, I think I've made you the victim through all these years. There's no easy way to say this, but after Blake, I never wanted another child I would be responsible for, because I knew deep inside it would devastate me if anything happened to him or her. To you. So what did I do? I made sure not to get too close to you." He stopped, unable to continue.

"Daddy, I never doubted you loved me."

"But did I show it? You always craved so much attention."

"Because you were my hero. And maybe because I have a little personality flaw. In case you haven't noticed, I tend to want my own way."

He was amazed by her understanding. Had she grown up while his back was turned? He covered her hands with his own, and in that moment, the light bulb went on. "You know, I'm wrong. After all these years, I've just realized something. Hell, it wasn't that I didn't want you. It was that I wanted you too much, but didn't feel I deserved anything good. And I was terrified something would go wrong again, as it had with Blake."

She squeezed his hand, then let go. "You don't have to tell me all of this."

"There's more. I said I didn't deserve anything good. That's the truth."

"What do you mean?"

"This is the hard part, honey. Something I hoped I would never have to tell you. Fathers want to be heroes in their daughters' eyes. But I did something in Vietnam that will cause you to think of me differently from now on."

"Please, Daddy, really. You don't—"

"Oh, but I do. The Vietnam War did strange things to those of us stationed in Southeast Asia. That's not an excuse, it's a fact. I missed your mother terribly and hadn't begun to deal with Blake's death. I looked in the wrong place for escape, comfort."

The color left her cheeks. "Drugs?"

"No." He looked directly at her. "There was a woman."

She sat back in her chair, staring at him, aghast. "I'm sorry. Say that again."

"I had an affair with an air force nurse."

"But Mom—"

"I never stopped loving your mother. But she was thousands of miles across the ocean. Diane was there. She was an oasis."

Lisa clapped her hands over her ears. "I don't need names."

He reached over and gently lowered her hands. Still clutching them, he said, "I'm afraid you do, honey. There's more."

"More?"

Tears moistened her eyes and he felt a stab of remorse. Neal had done to her what he had done to her mother. "Izzy has forgiven me. I hope you can. Especially when I tell you that I recently became aware that when Diane left Thailand, she was pregnant."

Lisa flapped her fingers in front of her eyes in an effort to regain control. "Wait. You're telling me you have another child?"

"I found out two weeks ago."

Abruptly she stood, as if searching for an escape route.

"Lisa!"

She wilted into her chair. "Brother or sister?"

"A brother. Mark Taylor is his name."

"I don't believe this."

"Please. Listen. It's time you knew about my father." Then he told her what his childhood had been like. "I never talked much about my dad, because, in important ways, I never really had a father after my mother died. I wish to God I had. So how can I blame Mark for trying to find his?"

Silence fell between them. "I love you and Jenny with all my heart, and I'll have to deal with your reactions to this news. But I want you to know one thing. I have more than enough love for all of you, Mark included."

"I'm trying to understand, Daddy, I really am, but this is hard."

"I knew it would be, but getting all this out in the open is the only honest thing to do."

There was little left to say. They threw away their cold cappuccinos, picked up the groceries and returned to the house in silence. Nothing had been settled and Sam was sick with regret.

Izzy and Scooter had finished the puzzle. When she looked up at him, her eyes clouded. His face must've told the story. In the tension-ridden atmosphere, Lisa stared at Izzy as if she had never seen her before. Izzy and Sam said their goodbyes. As they were leaving, Sam said, "Jenny and Don will know by this evening. Maybe you and your sister can talk."

On the drive to Colorado Springs, in as few words as possible, Sam relayed his conversation with Lisa. "It was awful, Iz. There's a chance she'll never forgive me."

"It was a lot for her to take in all at once."

"I know. But she was really hurt."

When they were on the southern edge of

Denver, a late-afternoon rainstorm descended, the perfect accompaniment to Sam's mood. He couldn't bear the thought of going through his confession again with Jenny. Splinters lodged in his gut. What good was it to gain a son if he lost his daughters.

Izzy put her hand on his knee, but kept her counsel. It was a long seventy-five miles to Colorado Springs.

From the depths of Sam's misery, he heard Izzy's cell phone ring. Pulling the phone from her purse, she answered, listened, and then without a word, handed it to Sam.

"Hello?"

"Daddy, it's me." Lisa's voice was an arrow to his heart. "I've been thinking. What we talked about today is pretty overwhelming. But I don't need to consult with Jenny, because there's one thing I know in this world. I have only one father, and I don't want to lose him." He heard her sniffle, and the next words come through sobs. "I love you, Daddy, no matter what, and I always will. You're my hero."

CHAPTER FOURTEEN

Breckenridge, Colorado

SAM AND I ARE home from Colorado Springs. I've
changed into my robe and slippers, crawled into
my chair, huddled under a blanket and am trying
to read, but I'm having trouble concentrating. The
emotions of the past few days undermined my
immune system. My throat is raw and my body
achy. Sam, on the other hand, has experienced a
burst of energy and is cleaning the storage room
off the garage.

Every time I try to focus on my book, the print
blurs and I see, instead, Jenny's face, contorted
with shock and incomprehension. Of my two
daughters, I'd expected Sam's news to be more
upsetting to Lisa, but Jenny went to pieces last
night. "How could you do that to Mother?" were
her exact words to Sam. "You weren't the only
one who had it tough, Dad. Mom was dealing
with a lot, too. She was taking care of me, her

parents, going to school. I remember how she'd flop into bed at night, sometimes too tired to read me a story. But never too tired to write you."

I'd tried to intervene, to calm her, but Sam held up his hand. "No, Izzy. I deserve every bit of this."

When Sam began talking about Diane and Mark, Jenny stormed out of the room, but not before she threw her parting shot. "The existence of this Mark person is enough. I don't need the sordid details. And have you thought about this? What am I supposed to tell my daughters about their grandfather?"

Don, concerned for Jenny, made his apologies and hurried after her.

Sam sank into a chair, defeated. "I didn't anticipate it would be this awful."

"Nor did I." We waited in pained silence, wondering if we should go after her. Fifteen minutes passed. Then our son-in-law reappeared.

"Jenny's pretty upset. This news came as a thunderbolt to both of us." His troubled eyes conveyed his concern. "I think you're going to have to be patient. If she can, Jenny needs to face this and get it behind her. But I have to tell you, it's shattered her illusions." Then, as if recalling his manners, he offered to get us drinks, but we declined. He stood awkwardly before excusing himself to rejoin his wife.

A succession of sneezes interrupts my reverie, and I dig in my pocket for a tissue. I don't like being sick. Clearly, though, I'm coming down with a bad cold. Once again I try the book and make it to the end of a chapter. But all the while I'm thinking about Jenny.

She had finally come back into the room, her face scrubbed of makeup and her eyes red. "Okay," she said with a big sigh, "I'm sorry, but I'm pretty emotional right now. I'm angry. I feel duped. And I'm disappointed. The whole idyllic childhood I thought I had was a myth."

I stopped her. "Jenny, it doesn't help to blow everything out of proportion. Very little of this affected your growing up. You were adored by both of us and what went on between your father and me didn't concern you then."

Sam's face was a mask. "All I can say is I'm sorry. Really sorry."

Jenny perched on the arm of the sofa. "I don't know what to think."

"You're supposed to think your parents are human. That no marriage is perfect. That we all have done things for which we need forgiveness." I pointed to Sam. "This is the same father you loved yesterday."

She avoided looking at either of us. "Do I have to meet this Mark?"

Sam lifted his head. "I'd like for you to. None of this is his fault any more than it's yours."

"Well, I don't know if I can do it." She'd stood and with a toss of her head said, "I'm going to bed. The guest room is made up for you. I'll see you at breakfast."

Sighing, I set my book on the end table and pick up my knitting. As if Orville has ESP, he comes into the room and bats at the yarn. I dangle a discarded strand and tease him with it. He's all leaps and paws. For him, it's a wonderful game.

We're in a game, too, and I don't know how it will all play out. This morning before we left Colorado Springs, Jenny apologized and gave us both hugs, but she never mentioned Mark. I know her. If she's decided she doesn't want to meet her half brother, it will be a tough sell. I appreciate her protectiveness of me, but she has scant understanding of how deeply I love her father or how much he and I need each other.

I haven't shared my concerns with Sam, since, in typical male fashion, he has taken her apology at face value. I sneeze violently, and Orville jumps two feet in the air, then scurries for safety. My head is throbbing. Abandoning the knitting, I go to the kitchen and take two aspirins, then trundle off to bed where not even worry about Jenny can keep me from drifting to sleep.

I'M AWAKENED BY A knock on the door. "Come in," I say drowsily.

Sam hands me the phone. "I thought you'd want to take this. It's Twink."

Struggling to a sitting position, I cradle the phone and lean back against the pillow. Sam discreetly leaves the room. "Hello, there."

"Did I wake you? Isn't it still daylight out there?"

"Yes and yes. But I'm so glad it's you. We've had big developments on the home front."

"Sam told me about Scooter. Poor little kid. How's Lisa bearing up?"

"She's been amazing. It hasn't hurt that a man has come into her life."

"Tell me more."

"Well, he's older, but seems very good for her."

Then with a throat that gets raspier as I talk, I fill her in on Mark's recent visit and our trips to tell the girls about their half brother.

"I thought Sam wasn't going to have anything to do with this guy."

"He changed his mind. Lisa's on board, but Jenny's another matter."

"She's jealous."

"Come again?"

"Yeah, she doesn't like it that Daddy strayed."

"You mean jealous on my account."

"No, no, my friend. She's jealous of this other woman who enchanted her daddy. You might have expected that from Lisa, but she's distracted by Mr. Wonderful. Besides, Lisa's a lot more intuitive than you give her credit for. Jenny has always thought her father walked on water whereas although Lisa wanted him to be a hero, she may have suspected he had flaws."

"You're scary, Twink. You almost make sense."

"You'll see. After Jenny thinks about it, she'll come around."

"I hope so."

"Now on to you, old childhood chum. How are you, aside, that is, from the ghastly cold?"

I sink further into the pillows. "I'm better. Getting the past out into the open has been a blessing."

"And Sam?"

"Oh, Twink, I have him back."

"And I know what that means, you lucky girl."

I don't tell her about the episode in the bus shelter or about Sam's willingness, after all these years, to talk about Blake. There are some things between a man and a wife that you don't share even with your best friend. "It means I love him even more than I did the night you told me to punt Drew Mayfield. It just gets better and better."

"Have you mastered the gazebo book yet?" she asks with a chortle.

I smile at her irreverence. "No, but we're working our way through it."

"I love you, Isabel."

"And I love you, Aurelia."

BEFORE DINNER, SAM fixes me a hot toddy and himself a scotch and water. Lying on the sofa under a blanket, I clutch a box of tissues and try to watch the news. He faces the television set, but doesn't seem to be following the news anchor.

"…the latest casualty reports from the Middle East…"

Sam turns to me. "Are you watching this?"

"Not really."

"Good." He picks up the remote and silences the TV. "I want to show you something and see what you think." From the legal pad on his chairside table, he pulls several folded sheets of paper. "While you were napping, I decided it might be a good idea to write the girls. I hit them suddenly and hard with my news. Maybe it would help if they had something in writing that they could read and keep. Here." He hands the letter to me. "They're essentially the same. See what you think."

I take a fortifying sip of my hot toddy, and open the first one.

Dear Jenny,

Yesterday evening, I knew what I had to tell

you would be very upsetting. I'm not proud of what happened in Thailand or of how my actions have hurt your mother and now you and your sister. I could tell you more about how Blake's death affected me and about the hell of war (and someday, should you ask, I will), but doing so now might lead you to believe I'm asking for your sympathy. I'm not. Committing adultery was wrong, no matter what the circumstances. But I can't undo the past. The question now is this: where do we go from here?

You, Lisa and Mark Taylor are all victims here. But you are all my children, as well. I pray we may come together as a family. Yes, that means I would like to include Mark to the extent he is willing and you and Lisa can welcome him. But if you decide that is too much to ask, I will not invite him to family gatherings.

Jenny, I have loved you since the moment your mother told me she was pregnant with you. I am proud of the woman you have become. You have a generous and caring heart. Please take the time you need to make a decision. Whatever the outcome, never doubt that I love you—I always have and always will.

After I finish the letter, both my nose and eyes are running. Between the lines, I read Sam's pain as well as his desire to bring his family together. Whether that can happen is out of our control. "In my opinion, it hits the right note."

"Not too groveling?"

"It's honest and direct and says just enough."

"How do you suppose the girls will react?"

I recall my conversation with Twink. "Trust your daughters, Sam. Give them time. Remember, they don't have a Montana fishing cabin to retreat to."

He grins sheepishly. "Low blow, woman."

"I think I'm entitled to one or two." I sneeze loudly into a tissue.

"I can't argue with that, it's just—"

"It's not easy waiting."

"No, it isn't." Then he hands me another letter. "This one is for Mark." Sam sits with his hands folded in his lap while I read what he has written.

Dear Mark,
It occurs to me that you might have interpreted my delay in agreeing to meet you as a denial of your mother and the relationship we shared. I think it's important for you to know that I found your mother to be one of the gentlest, most sensitive, genuinely good people I have ever met. What she gave me in

the midst of my personal turmoil was loving, nonjudgmental understanding. The fact that she never revealed my identity to you shows how much she valued my well-being and the well-being of my family. I hope that whatever hurt I inflicted on her disappeared when she married Rolf Taylor and that she had a happy, fulfilling life.

What a joy you must have been to her! You share her sensitivity and goodness, and I give your mother and Rolf great credit for the man you've become.

That having been said, Izzy and I would like to invite you and your family to be as much a part of our lives as you would choose to be. I can't yet speak for our daughters Lisa and Jenny, who, as I'm sure you can understand, have been thrown for a loop by this turn of events. Please take your time to discuss this with your family. We look forward to hearing from you.

"Well?" Sam says as I lay the letter in my lap.

"It's quite good, except you've left out something very important."

"What's that?"

"Telling Mark you loved his mother." Sam turns to me in astonishment, but I hurry on. "Because you did, Sam. You did. In your own way, in that long-ago time and chaotic place. I admit when I first learned of your infidelity, I was hurt, angry, jealous, you name it. But as I've thought about it, I'm thankful that Diane Berrigan was there to save you. Because that's what she did. She must have loved you very much to sacrifice as she did. That is a thing to be honored. Mark needs to know."

Sam's eyes shine with unshed tears. "My Izzy," he says, wonderingly, more to himself than to me. "You are something else."

A FAIRLY UNEVENTFUL week passes. I'm rummaging in the attic storage space for our Halloween decorations when I hear the phone. Sam's playing golf, so I run into his office to pick up. "Hey, Mom, it's Lisa." As if I wouldn't recognize my own daughter's voice.

"I was hoping you'd call with an update on Scooter."

"He's much better. The challenge is keeping him quiet. Because of the concussion, he's not supposed to be too active yet. But Hank's helping with that."

"Oh?"

"He comes over after work every day and you ought to see the two of them. Building models, playing video games, working together on Scooter's homework. I don't know how I'd manage without him."

"Hank must be a real kid person."

"His own children are grown. He claims he's enjoying the way being with Scooter is bringing out his inner child again."

"Have you met his children?"

"Just before Scooter's accident, we had dinner with the daughter that lives here, and I've spoken on the phone with his son in Phoenix."

"What's their reaction to you?"

"Oh, Mom, I was so nervous, but the dinner went really well. Janine, that's the daughter, told me in the powder room that her dad had been really lonely for a long time and that she was glad he'd found someone."

"What about the son?"

"He sounded darling. He said, 'Hey, Lisa, you must be really something if you got the old man out of his recliner.'"

In Lisa's voice I hear a lightness that does a mother's heart good. "This could be promising."

"It is. I'm so happy, Mom, I almost have to pinch myself. I was pretty much of a pill before Hank came along."

I decline to agree, relieved that she is in a better place now. "It's great that Hank and Scooter get along so well."

"Yeah, it is. Hey, is Daddy handy?"

"He's at the golf course."

"Darn, I wanted to tell him how much I appreciated his letter. It made me cry." She hesitated, then went on. "Do you think it would be okay if I wrote Mark?"

Okay? Angels sing hosannas in my head. "It would be a lovely and generous gesture. Your father will be delighted."

"I got to thinking after I met Hank's children and liked them so much. Family isn't limited, you know what I mean? We have love enough to go around to everybody."

Acceptance coming from the least expected source. Life is full of surprises. "I'm in your father's study. I can give you the address now."

As I'm reading it off to her, I wonder about Jenny, who has called a couple of times without saying one word about Sam's letter or Mark. I tiptoe into the subject. "Have you talked with your sister?"

"About Mark?"

"Yes."

"Uh, Mom, she's having a hard time. I think she's going to have to work through it on her own. I've told her how I feel, but she isn't there yet."

"Just wondering."

"One other thing, Mom. Daddy's seventieth

birthday is coming up the weekend after Thanksgiving. We should throw him a big party."

I've been so preoccupied I haven't even thought about Sam's birthday. "You're right. He'd probably enjoy that."

"How about if we have it at your house, but you leave all the details to Jenny and me. We want this to be a celebration for you both. We'll figure out the invitations, food, party favors, stuff like that. All you and Daddy have to do is show up."

Lisa is on a roll. "Okay. Consider it a deal."

When Sam gets home from golfing and I tell him the birthday plan, he claps a hand to his forehead in mock horror. "Seventy? Who, me?" Then he hugs me tight. "Amazing, isn't it? At seventy I have more to celebrate than ever."

Breckenridge, Colorado

BEFORE EVERYONE ARRIVES for Sam's birthday party, I have a quiet few minutes to myself. My journal lies on the dresser. So much has happened since I last wrote in it, and my heart is full. I pick it up and carry it into the family room where I settle in my chair. With Sally for company, Sam is outside sweeping the front porch and walkway. Orville suns himself on the windowsill overlooking the bird feeders. Laying my head back, I close my eyes, savoring the peace and quiet.

Shortly I pick up a pen and begin writing in my new journal, the one I will pass on to my girls. I'm keeping the other one for myself. It's been a wonderful help in sorting out my life, but I doubt a mother should share her intimate secrets with her children.

My darling daughters, I don't know exactly when you will be reading this. Probably after I'm long gone. You need to know that, much as I love you, there are some things that are very difficult to share with one's children.

Despite my initial resistance, I've gotten in the habit of recording life's ups and downs, and I intend to continue. Reviewing the past, I have come to the conclusion that life is unpredictable, and rare are the moments when everything is exactly as you think you want it to be. I say as you "think" you want it to be, because sometimes the outcomes you desire are ones that limit you. And the experiences that seem so trying at the moment can be the very ones from which you learn and grow.

I know I'm waxing philosophical. Forgive me. But in the midst of life are situations that turn out well—like your father's finally ex-

pressing his grief about Blake and acknowl-
edging Mark as his son—and then there are
others that may be forever unresolved, like
Jenny's difficulty accepting her father's
shortcomings. But there is a great deal of
love in this family, and where there's love,
there is always hope.

"Izzy?" Sam sticks his head in the door. "Come
quick. Our first guest is arriving."

Closing the journal, I cast around for a place to
put it. Then I light upon the perfect spot. Beneath
the billiken.

Satisfied, I move to the door where I am
stunned to see Twink, dressed flamboyantly in a
purple dress, mounting the porch steps. I can
hardly speak. "How? When—?"

She holds out her arms. "My friend, you have
spectacular daughters. They said I couldn't miss
Sam's party, so here I am."

When I step into her embrace, the years melt
away. "I've missed you."

"And me, you, too."

Sam walks toward us, beaming, and we break
apart. "Hey, Miss Aurelia, Miss Isabel, let's get
this party going!"

Over Twink's shoulder I see two more vehicles

arriving. Soon the house will be filled with the people I love best in all the world.

As we walk toward the driveway to greet the others, Sam slips an arm around my shoulder and pulls me close. "You wouldn't have been nearly as happy with that Drew fella."

I stop and drape my arms around his neck and say in my best Mae West imitation, "Have I made it worth your while, big boy?" Then I lay a big birthday kiss on him for all the world to see.

"Oh, my God!" Twink shrieks. "The gazebo book has come to life!"

As Jenny and Lisa and their families approach, they have no idea why Twink and I are dissolved in laughter. Nor does Sam.

When all is said and done, it's nice still to have a secret or two.

EPILOGUE

Breckenridge, Colorado
Late November

ALTHOUGH MARK HAD MADE the drive to Breckenridge twice before, returning with his family was special. He pointed to a ski run carved from an evergreen slope. "Someday, boys, maybe you can learn to ski."

From the backseat came enthusiastic responses. "I saw these guys on TV do that" and "I bet I'd be really good."

Beside him, Sue patted his leg. "Nervous?"

"A little. This is a pretty big deal."

"Are we there yet?" Cole asked.

The parents laughed at the cliché. "Almost," Mark said, aware of the buzz of excitement in his chest.

"I never met a new grandpa and grandma before." This from Cody. "What should I call them?"

"Why don't you ask them?" Mark replied, wondering if he'd made too big a deal of Sam's birthday party invitation.

"Izzy. That's a funny name."

"I've heard about Uncle Sam, but not Grandpa Sam."

The boys' chatter took them to the house where several other vehicles were already parked. Pulling the car to a stop, Mark took a deep breath. "Okay, guys. Let's go meet the Lamberts."

Sue tucked her hand reassuringly in his as the boys bounded for the front door, the place he'd stood with his heart in his throat only a few short weeks ago.

Before he could ring the bell, Isabel Lambert opened the door—an astonished smile lighting her face. "I couldn't believe it when I saw you coming up the walk!" Her glance swept from Mark, to Sue, to the boys. "This is the best birthday surprise ever!" Then she gave hugs all around, and to their credit, the boys didn't shy away. "Please, please, come in. Sam will be so happy." Izzy put an arm around Sue and ushered them all into the family room.

Over the mantel a banner proclaimed "Happy 70th." Balloons and crepe paper streamers hung from the ceiling. "Everybody!" Izzy clapped her hands. "Look who's here."

Carrying drinks, Sam entered from the kitchen. His eyes locked on Mark's, and without missing a beat, he handed the drinks to an older woman in a purple dress and rushed across the room to engulf his son in a bear hug.

"Happy birthday, Sam."

He held Mark at arm's length. "I'm flabbergasted. I had no idea you were coming, but it makes the celebration perfect."

He kissed Sue on the cheek and then knelt down to the boys' level. "Which of you is Cody and which is Cole?"

"He is," they giggled, pointing to each other.

Mark placed a hand first on Cole's head. "This is Cole."

"Glad to meet you." Sam shook the boy's hand before turning to his twin. "So you must be Cody."

"Can we call you Grandpa Sam?" Cole asked.

Sam hesitated, as if seeking Mark's permission. "By all means."

Izzy spirited Sue off, and a dark-haired young woman came over to Mark and gave him a hug. "I'm Lisa," she told him. "I've enjoyed your e-mails. Thank you so much for making the effort to be here." Then she addressed the boys. "Ready to meet your cousin Scooter?" They trailed her across the room to a little guy about their age wearing a Denver Broncos sweatshirt.

Sam clapped a hand on Mark's shoulder and led him to the kitchen where he fixed him a drink. Arm in arm, Izzy and Sue joined them, chatting like old friends. "I'm dumbfounded," Sam said. "Did you arrange this reunion, Izzy?"

"I most certainly did not. I'm as surprised as you...and equally delighted."

"Well, who...?"

Just then an attractive well-dressed blonde came into the room. Her eyes lighted on Sam with such love Mark had to avert his gaze to keep from feeling like an intruder. She put her arms around their father and said with a hitch in her voice, "Happy birthday, Daddy!"

Sam held her close, then looked questioningly at her. "Jenny?" He fumbled for words. "You? You did this?"

"I did. After talking with Lisa and doing some heavy thinking about what's really important to me, I called Mark and invited him and his family to join us today. It was a way to show you how much I love you." She stepped back, and for the first time, acknowledged Mark with a nod. "It took me a while, but I finally decided I was being petty and selfish. You know, Daddy, I've missed Blakie all these years, too. When I thought about it, I realized that what was stopping me from accepting Mark was that I didn't want any replacement brother." She cast a baleful glance in Mark's direction. "Sorry."

He touched her shoulder. "I understand. I never

expected instant acceptance. Let's start out getting to know one another. Just being friends."

"I'd like that."

"So would I," Sam added quietly. "Thank you, Jenny. And thank you, Mark, for bringing your wonderful family."

During the cocktail hour, Sue and Mark mingled with the others, asking and answering questions, discovering shared interests and gradually feeling more and more as if they belonged. He observed the pride Sam took in each person there, the loving way he caught Izzy's eye every now and then, as if affirming their connection.

Lisa nudged him in the ribs. "Do you see what I see?" She gestured toward the fireplace where the lady in the purple dress and Sam's air force buddy were deep in conversation. "Is it my imagination or are there sparks flying over there?"

"They do look pretty engrossed. Tell me again who she is."

"Mom's best friend from forever. Twink. And that's Daddy's friend Mike. He has a cabin in Montana. Dad goes there to fish. Hey, we've had one happy ending today, but I don't see any reason to stop there, do you?"

"What's this about happy endings?" Hank slipped up behind Lisa and wrapped his arms around her waist.

"I believe in them," Lisa said, looking up adoringly.

Needing a moment to himself, Mark stepped to the large picture window. The setting sun cast purple shadows on the mountains and flamed the sky with orange and magenta. The grandeur of the heavens matched the depth of his emotions. Originally, he'd come to this beautiful place searching for a father. But he'd found a family.

Lost in thought, he was startled when he felt a gentle hand on his sleeve. "Mark, are you all right?"

Izzy stood beside him, studying the panorama before them.

"I'm finding it's pretty emotional trying to take everything in."

"It's often like that when love is involved."

"I'd like to bottle this moment and treasure it forever."

"Can't be done," she said, turning toward him and placing the strangest object in his hands. About four inches high, it was a Buddha-like figurine with the happiest, smug grin on his impish face.

"What's this?" he asked.

"The billiken my grandmother gave me."

"Billiken?"

"That's what he's called. He's a talisman. Look on the bottom."

Mark turned the statue over and in the failing light read the inscribed words. *The god of things as they ought to be.*

"When my grandmother gave him to me, she said that every now and then things are, indeed, exactly as they ought to be."

He cupped the billiken in his hand, marveling. "Like now?"

Izzy's answering smile was radiant. "Like now, son."

* * * * *

Turn the page for a sneak preview of
AFTERSHOCK,
a new anthology featuring New York Times
bestselling author Sharon Sala.

Available October 2008.

n✹cturne™

Dramatic and sensual tales
of paranormal romance.

Chapter 1

October
New York City

Nicole Masters was sitting cross-legged on her sofa while a cold autumn rain peppered the windows of her fourth-floor apartment. She was poking at the ice cream in her bowl and trying not to be in a mood.

Six weeks ago, a simple trip to her neighborhood pharmacy had turned into a nightmare. She'd walked into the middle of a robbery. She never even saw the man who shot her in the head and left her for dead. She'd survived, but some of her senses had not. She was dealing with short-term memory loss and a tendency to stagger. Even though she'd been told the problems were most likely temporary, she waged a daily battle with depression.

Her parents had been killed in a car wreck when she was twenty-one. And except for a few friends—and most recently her boyfriend, Dominic Tucci, who lived in the apartment right above hers, she was alone. Her doctor kept reminding her that she should be grateful to be alive, and on one level she knew he was right. But he wasn't living in her shoes.

If she'd been anywhere else but at that pharmacy when the robbery happened, she wouldn't have died twice on the way to the hospital. Instead of being grateful that she'd survived, she couldn't stop thinking of what she'd lost.

But that wasn't the end of her troubles. On top of everything else, something strange was happening inside her head. She'd begun to hear odd things: sounds, not voices—at least, she didn't think it was voices. It was more like the distant noise of rapids—a rush of wind and water inside her head that, when it came, blocked out everything around her. It didn't happen often, but when it did, it was frightening, and it was driving her crazy.

The blank moments, which is what she called them, even had a rhythm. First there came that sound, then a cold sweat, then panic with no reason. Part of her feared it was the beginning of an emotional breakdown. And part of her feared it wasn't—that it was going to turn out to be a permanent souvenir of her resurrection.

Frustrated with herself and the situation as it stood, she upped the sound on the TV remote.

But instead of *Wheel of Fortune,* an announcer broke in with a special bulletin.

"This just in. Police are on the scene of a kidnapping that occurred only hours ago at The Dakota. Molly Dane, the six-year-old daughter of one of Hollywood's blockbuster stars, Lyla Dane, was taken by force from the family apartment. At this time they have yet to receive a ransom demand. The house-keeper was seriously injured during the abduction, and is, at the present time, in surgery. Police are hoping to be able to talk to her once she regains consciousness. In the mean-time, we are going now to a press conference with Lyla Dane."

Horrified, Nicole stilled as the cameras went live to where the actress was speaking before a bank of microphones. The shock and terror in Lyla Dane's voice were physically painful to watch. But even though Nicole kept upping the volume, the sound continued to fade.

Just when she was beginning to think something was wrong with her set, the broadcast suddenly switched from the Dane press conference to what appeared to be footage of the kidnapping, begin-ning with footage from inside the apartment.

When the front door suddenly flew back against the wall and four men rushed in, Nicole gasped. Horrified, she quickly realized that this must have been caught on a security camera inside the Dane apartment.

As Nicole continued to watch, a small Asian woman, who she guessed was the maid, rushed forward in an effort to keep them out. When one of the men hit her in the face with his gun, Nicole moaned. The violence was too reminiscent of what she'd lived through. Sick to her stomach, she fisted her hands against her belly, wishing it was over, but unable to tear her gaze away.

When the maid dropped to the carpet, the same man followed with a vicious kick to the little woman's midsection that lifted her off the floor.

"Oh, my God," Nicole said. When blood began to pool beneath the maid's head, she started to cry.

As the tape played on, the four men split up in different directions. The camera caught one running down a long marble hallway, then disappearing into a room. Moments later he reappeared, carrying a little girl, who Nicole assumed was Molly Dane. The child was wearing a pair of red pants and a white turtleneck sweater, and her hair was partially blocking her abductor's face as he carried her down the hall. She was kicking and screaming in his arms, and when he slapped her, it elicited an agonized scream that brought the other three running. Nicole watched in horror as one of them ran up and put his hand over Molly's face. Seconds later, she went limp.

One moment they were in the foyer, then they were gone.

Nicole jumped to her feet, then staggered drunkenly. The bowl of ice cream she'd absentmindedly placed in her lap shattered at her feet, splattering glass and melting ice cream everywhere.

The picture on the screen abruptly switched from the kidnapping to what Nicole assumed was a rerun of Lyla Dane's plea for her daughter's safe return, but she was numb.

Before she could think what to do next, the doorbell rang. Startled by the unexpected sound, she shakily swiped at the tears and took a step forward. She didn't feel the glass shards piercing her feet until she took the second step. At that point, sharp pains shot through her foot. She gasped, then looked down in confusion. Her legs looked as if she'd been running through mud, and she was standing in broken glass and ice cream, while a thin ribbon of blood seeped out from beneath her toes.

"Oh, no," Nicole mumbled, then stifled a second moan of pain.

The doorbell rang again. She shivered, then clutched her head in confusion.

"Just a minute!" she yelled, then tried to sidestep the rest of the debris as she hobbled to the door.

When she looked through the peephole in the door, she didn't know whether to be relieved or regretful.

It was Dominic, and as usual, she was a mess.

Nicole smiled a little self-consciously as she opened the door to let him in. "I just don't know what's happening to me. I think I'm losing my mind."

"Hey, don't talk about my woman like that."

Nicole rode the surge of delight his words brought. "So I'm still your woman?"

Dominic lowered his head.

Their lips met.

The kiss proceeded.

Slowly.

Thoroughly.

* * * * *

Be sure to look for the AFTERSHOCK
*anthology next month, as well as
other exciting paranormal stories
from Silhouette Nocturne.
Available in October wherever books are sold.*

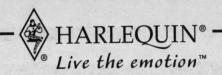

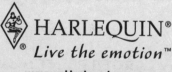

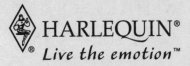

HARLEQUIN®
INTRIGUE®

BREATHTAKING ROMANTIC SUSPENSE

Shared dangers and passions lead to electrifying
romance and heart-stopping suspense!

Every month, you'll meet six new heroes
who are guaranteed to make your spine tingle
and your pulse pound. With them you'll enter
into the exciting world of Harlequin Intrigue—
where your life is on the line
and so is your heart!

THAT'S INTRIGUE—
ROMANTIC SUSPENSE
AT ITS BEST!

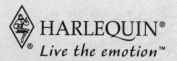

HARLEQUIN®
Live the emotion™

Harlequin® Historical
Historical Romantic Adventure!

*Imagine a time of chivalrous
knights and unconventional ladies,
roguish rakes and impetuous
heiresses, rugged cowboys
and spirited frontierswomen—
these rich and vivid tales will
capture your imagination!*

*Harlequin Historical...
they're too good to miss!*

HHDIR06

HARLEQUIN®
Presents

**The world's bestselling romance series...
The series that brings you your favorite authors,
month after month:**

Helen Bianchin...Emma Darcy
Lynne Graham...Penny Jordan
Miranda Lee...Sandra Marton
Anne Mather...Carole Mortimer
Melanie Milburne...Michelle Reid

and many more talented authors!

Wealthy, powerful, gorgeous men...
Women who have feelings just like your own...
The stories you love, set in exotic, glamorous locations...

HARLEQUIN®
Presents

Seduction and Passion Guaranteed!